RIVER OF HOPE

Roger Granelli was born and bred in Wales, and educated at the University of Warwick and Cardiff University. He is a writer, a professional musician, and a landscape photographer.

He has published a novella and ten novels in various genres and styles, including the Palermo stories, depicting organised crime, and the Mark Richards trilogy, featuring a petty criminal turned private eye. His first novel, *Crystal Spirit,* was set in the Welsh Valleys and Spain during the civil war. He has won three writing awards for his work, and contributed numerous short stories to magazines and radio. His collected stories, *Any Kind of Broken Man*, with a foreword by Phil Rickman, were published by Cockatrice Books in 2022.

RIVER OF HOPE

ROGER GRANELLI

Cockatrice Books
Y diawl a'm llaw chwith

River of Hope by Roger Granelli was first published by Cockatrice Books in 2023.

Editor: Rob Mimpriss
www.cockatrice-books.com
mail@cockatrice-books.com

The author gratefully acknowledges Eltham Jones, who suggested the title.

I was curious about Schweitzer. I had been since I first arrived on the west coast of Africa. As we approached Cape Lopez, Gabon had loomed up out of a shimmering heat haze, in a mix of swirling greens and browns slowly firming up. When I could see land clearly, I knew a great part of my future was opening up before me. It had to, for I had gambled everything I had to be here.

Schweitzer had been pointed out to me once, stalking the docks of Cape Lopez. He was quite a tall man, in a white suit and broad-brimmed hat, about forty years old, but looking older. He had a fine head of silvering hair, and the type of build that was a challenge to any rash wind. I didn't approach him then, but felt that our paths would cross one day, and so it came to pass, a few years later.

We approached Lambaréné in late afternoon. A low sun was sinking beneath the green dome of the jungle. It fanned its last rays of light over the river, and turned sluggish grey water silver. Sunlight changed from a blinding white to a yellow haze, and flies clustered over the water in dark clouds. They seemed crazed by the dying of the light, black battalions rising and falling in hysterical formation.

Unperturbed, my men pulled on their paddles, standing upright in the dugout. They were so skilful in their work that our progress barely disturbed the surface of the water. There was just a soft, rhythmical swish as we moved upstream. I sat in the rear of the boat and smoked cheap cigars, one after another, to keep the flies away.

We sighted Schweitzer's mission at sunset. I wanted to arrive late in the day, just before the light faded, and it disappeared very quickly here. This would stop the people at Lambaréné fussing too much, for my presence on the river often made the locals excited.

My reputation often went before me, and some here took exception to my activities, missionaries especially. But I had been told that Schweitzer was different. They said that he took a more measured view of such things, though I still expected to be lectured on the perils of drink.

I would soon find out what kind of man Schweitzer was, for I had a few days to kill before my steamer could get back up the Ogowe river. It had busted its screw chewing up the flank of a hippo, and was in dry dock at Cape Lopez.

Before it could be fixed I had to wait for Jan Pieters to sober up, which took days. Nothing could be rushed here, but

I was used to this now. Sometimes *mañana* never came at all. The climate did not support rush, and time in Gabon moved as listlessly as the Ogowe.

Pieters was a Flemish Belgian, whom I drank with for a while, until he became too belligerent when in his cups. Like so many who came here, Pieters had chased after illusory fortunes, but after a series of wrong moves, he had resigned himself to boat repairs and occasional welding work at the docks on the coast. At least that gave him some kind of a living.

Pieters was a good welder and would fix the bent screw, but he was an even better drunk. I think he was determined to be a character sprung from the pages of a Joseph Conrad novel, whisky-soaked, bitter and lost. Not that the man had ever heard of Conrad.

Most of Schweitzer's people were elsewhere as the dug-out glided smoothly to a sandy shore. Landing places like this were rare on the Ogowe. Usually the jungle came right to the water's edge, as if in competition with it. Roots became entangled in the banking in crazy disarray, and some were thicker than a man's midriff.

The river itself was a very disorderly affair. It had countless run-offs that led who knows where. Much of the interior here was still unknown to whites. It would be easy to take my steamboat up the wrong tributary, one that might prove shallow enough to rip open her hull.

My pilot skills had improved in the last few years, but I still had to draw on the expert knowledge of my headman Julius from time to time. At least my steamer, the *River Ghost*, was not a cumbersome paddleboat. The *Alemba*, the official

French riverboat here, had two paddles side by side, and was far less mobile than the *Ghost*.

My men did not like Lambaréné. They were afraid of leprosy and God knows what else their minds could conjure up about this place. Julius spoke in low whispers and slapped one man when he began to roll his eyes and talk about evil spirits. Julius turned to me proudly.

'I settle him down good, boss,' he said, but then he too grew nervous.

*

Another of Hope's crew approached Julius when the boss was out of earshot.

'Why do you suck up to him like that?' Osobu asked.

Julius had to concentrate hard to understand the man. There were so many languages in his country but most tried to communicate in Fang, and some French. Osobu only had a basic command of Fang, plus a few essential French phrases he'd picked up from Hope.

'Mind your own business and get back to work,' Julius said.

'It's dangerous here.'

'Don't talk like an ignorant country boy.'

Osobu tensed and Julius saw his muscular arms flex.

'I saw fear in your eyes too,' Osobu said, 'but you think you are better than us because boss man has made you number one boy.'

'Shut up now.'

Julius stood eyeball to eyeball with Osobu. They were tall, well-built men and it was tense moment before Osobu turned away with a scowl and a shrug.

Julius watched Hope stroll up towards the settlement. He liked this white man, up to a point, but Osobu's words hit home. He felt he was caught in the middle of two cultures, his own and that of the whites here, in *his* land. Julius was the first in his family to learn to read and write French, but Hope did not know this. Very few did, for it was not wise to show anyone you were too clever here, not if you were black.

*

A tall, thin man was approaching us with a friendly smile, but when he waved an arm in greeting it was obvious that his hand had fused into a solid ball of flesh. If he still had fingers they were not visible. I waved back and to the relief of my rowers the man did not come any closer.

My men were coastal dwellers, and whilst fine on the steamer, they did not like getting up this close with the heart of the country. People had warred here through the ages, like everywhere else in the world. The man with the ruined hand pointed me towards the main buildings of Lambaréné.

I told Julius to stay with the men, and to keep order. He was my makeshift sergeant, and like all good sergeants he commanded the right mix of respect, fear and hatred from the crew. Why not, for I had been his role model.

I surveyed Schweitzer's world. Lambaréné was an amazing place. It had been hacked out of the primeval forest, six hundred yards of vulnerable white man's presence, barely clinging on, but quietly impressive for all that. It said something about Schweitzer. This place made a statement, and it spoke of commitment and resolve.

A cluster of nondescript but sturdy-looking buildings spread out over a small piece of land surrounded by jungle. A stream ran down the hillside to feed into a small lake, and if you peered through the haze of the late afternoon, it was possible to see a fringe of blue hills in the distance. All in all it was as good a spot as any for a mission and a hospital.

Lambaréné was built on three hills. One corrugated metal building and a collection of smaller bamboo dwellings dotted the area, some in obvious need of repair. Schweitzer's mission was obviously a work in progress, but the war would have interrupted his life here.

I suddenly remembered that Schweitzer was a German, though I had read somewhere that he was more French these days. He was also married, and I couldn't imagine what it must be like for his wife in this climate. A European woman in the interior of the country was a rarity indeed, and I looked forward to meeting her. In fact I looked forward to meeting both of them, so desperate was I for some decent conversation.

Guided by the man with stumps for hands I walked up to the largest building. It was propped up off the ground by a series of iron piles, all the better to protect it from the elements.

Schweitzer himself appeared on a veranda, in the same white flannels I'd seen in Cape Lopez. How the hell did he keep them so clean? He wore a thin black bow tie, which made me think of Charlie Chaplin, though I doubted that would amuse Schweitzer.

The doctor had put on weight since that time I'd seen him at the docks, and was rather thickset now. His figure caught the dying of the light and for a moment sunlight seemed trapped in his silvering hair. If I *had* been a believer I might have thought there really was something Godlike about the man.

'You are a welcome visitor, sir,' Schweitzer said in English, with just the hint of a German accent.

'How did you know I wasn't French?' I said.

'You are Adam Hope, the Englishman. I was told you were back on the Ogowe, and without your boat too.'

Schweitzer had got my name right, if not the nationality.

I took his hand, which was almost cool, and firm in its grip. We locked eyes for a moment, and his look was appraising, but not judgmental. I thought this surprising for a man of God, considering my recent history. Most of the God-fearing men I'd met in my time had never seemed very full of Christian charity to me. They were usually puffed up with religious vanity, or at least an annoying smugness. Schweitzer was different. He had the look of someone convinced his life was on the right path, and took strength from it, without the need to drive others down the same road.

Schweitzer swept me up to his house with an expansive hand. It was a solid looking building, and the metal piles had kept it from the worst of the jungle rot. As I entered, a last flicker of light reddened the rust on its corrugated roof.

I could smell cooking. It smelt like roast lamb, but it couldn't be, not here. It made my stomach lurch with the need to be fed, but also with childhood memories.

'Come in,' Schweitzer said, 'come in, before God's creatures start biting. Your men will be given food and shelter.'

I was immediately struck by the piano in the main room. It was a black upright that dominated the space around it. An oil lamp rested on it, and sheaves of yellowing music manuscripts were scattered all about the room.

'That took some getting here,' I said, nodding towards the piano.

'Indeed. It came upriver on the *Alemba* in a zinc-lined case, and then was brought to the shore in a dugout, would you believe? Watching that was quite nerve-wracking for me. It looked like an ancient sarcophagus being delivered to a pharaoh's tomb. That was quite a journey for a piano from Paris, but the effort was well worth it, Mr. Hope. I managed to tune it myself.'

Schweitzer tapped the piano like it was a favoured child. 'This is my indulgence, an echo of my former life if you like. It was bought for me by kind friends back home, and built by them too, in a way to help it to better withstand the conditions here.'

Schweitzer ran a hand through some of the music placed on the piano in a thick pile.

'Manuscripts age so quickly in this climate,' he murmured, as he held one up.

I ached for a drink, for my last one had been more than two days ago. Good whisky was just a memory these days, but anything would have done at this moment, even the stuff I sold to the locals.

I was a trader in timber who used liquor to buy it, but I had started to branch out in the last year, to include anything else that might turn a good profit. Sometimes I brought European goods to the small pockets of whites here, but mainly it was just liquor, usually rum, sometimes poor quality whisky, when I could get it.

I was continuing the time-honoured tradition of the white man in selling worthless goods to people of more innocent worlds, usually after they had been subjugated with a fair amount of slaughter in the name of civilization. I wasn't proud of it, but at least I did not steal their lands or ravish their womenfolk. Looking at Schweitzer, the piano, the books, and small cross on the wall, I knew this had to be a dry place.

'There will be tea in a few minutes,' Schweitzer said with a smile, as if divining my thoughts, 'and then a meal when we are ready.'

A servant called Joseph served the tea. He entered the room noiselessly, a slight man who smiled shyly and brought in green tea, to be served in white china cups. I watched Joseph pour the tea from an ornate teapot, obviously something brought from the old country.

I sat at the slightly unsteady table with Schweitzer and steamed in the heat, for the night brought no relief here. The temperature might lessen somewhat, but in its place came a punishing humidity. This was Conrad's world indeed.

The atmosphere at Lambaréné hung heavy as lead this night, and was fusty with the forest that lay all around it. Decay and rebirth appeared to be in a race here. Nature seemed to speed up, as if drunk on its own power. I sipped the refreshing tea and watched a rag-sized moth flutter against the wire mesh window.

'I am still not really used to this climate,' Schweitzer said. 'I have been here some years year now, off and on, but it is still hard for me. You do not seem much affected by it, Mr. Hope?'

'I was at first, but I've been here long enough to cope. One becomes accustomed to it, up to a point. Your blood adjusts to the new environment. Mine did anyway.'

There were a few more minutes of polite but rather vacuous chat that took me back to another world. I almost expected a green sward to appear before me, and cucumber sandwiches to be served on it. My mind wandered for a moment.

Laura had been so proud of me going off to war in my second lieutenant's uniform, but I knew she was also desperate for me to survive. Most of the war women had been torn like that. Pride and fear combined to mix into some strange new emotion, until it became a kind of national unease. They gave white feathers to those who did not fight, and broke their hearts over those who did.

I survived, but my relationship with Laura did not. I could not go back to a normal life, for I had lost the ability to do so. All such notions were burnt out of me by the war, and Laura had got tired of waiting anyway. I heard that she married a man in her father's business a year after the war ended. He shipped coal from the docks of Cardiff, some of which had even got as far as Cape Lopez, and into the belly of my steamer. Laura's father thought she was well rid of me. The man was also a business rival of my father's, which added a little spice to the situation.

'Lost in your thoughts, Mr. Hope?'

'I'm sorry, Doctor, that's very rude of me.'

'No, not at all. Just between ourselves, I do it myself in company from time to time.'

More hopeful pleading by my stomach was finally rewarded by a fine meal, again served by Joseph, whom Schweitzer described as 'one of his helpers,' though servant seemed more appropriate in my eyes.

Joseph brought us a tureen of fish stew, plus *domada*, one of my favourite local dishes, an untidy mess of peanuts and whatever vegetables the cook could find, garnished with a mix of herbs to enhance the flavour. When I first arrived on the coast I found the food here exotic, especially after four years of trench rations. Any Parisian chef would have been impressed by Gabonese cuisine.

As poor as this French colony was, Gabon was in better shape than many in Africa. That was one of the things that had attracted me. I also had a fair grasp of French, which was a great help in getting my business set up. What could be better for the authorities here than an allied *war hero* who spoke French, a man bringing fresh investment?

Schweitzer seemed to enjoy watching me eat, though I tried to rein in my hunger to polite levels. My host ate rather sparingly but insisted that Joseph heap more onto my plate. When I was sated and the meal over, I was invited back into what I thought must be his inner sanctum, an untidy, paper-strewn sitting room-cum-office, dominated by the piano as centrepiece.

We stayed up for a while longer, the doctor smoking his pipe, but not talking much. I used up my last Cuban cigar in honour of my visit, sucking in as much of the fine smoke as my lungs could take. I put my head back in the chair and exhaled a long stream of blue-grey smoke. It added to the small tobacco cloud that already nestled under the ceiling. It would be back to cheap smokes for me in the morning.

Schweitzer remained silent, and our lack of talk was getting rather marked. I asked him what he played on his piano.

'Bach,' he said, as if talking to the sheet music rather than me, 'it's nearly always Bach for me, J.S. Bach of course. He's my other god, you might say.' Schweitzer chuckled. 'I hope that doesn't sound sacrilegious.'

'No, of course not.'

'Bach has been very good to me,' Schweitzer murmured, 'very good indeed. I trained on the organ, you know, and Bach was the centre of my musical world then, and he still is now. In a way he is responsible for my being here.'

'How is that, Doctor?'

'I wrote a book about him, and people bought it. An amazing number of people, really, and the royalties I received partly funded our journey here.'

'So, you are a musician and a writer as well as a doctor? A man of many parts.'

A thin smile appeared on his serious face, but only for a moment.

'If you like,' Schweitzer said. 'I am a theologian too. Apparently, they call me a polymath now, a term first coined by a German, by the way, many years ago.'

Schweitzer pulled at his thick moustache as few times as he paused.

'You are a single man, I take it, Mr. Hope?'

'I am.'

'I am blessed with a wife and a daughter, but they are not here, not this time. Helene was with me when I first arrived at Lambaréné. She was a great help in starting the hospital and mission, my rock, you might say. During the war we were interned in France, so I thought it would be best for her to stay behind this time. I knew that a lot of what we had originally achieved here would have fallen into disrepair. So much work was undone and I had to begin again, as it were.'

'I'm disappointed that I can't meet her.'

'Maybe someday you will, if you stay out here long enough.'

'I have no plans to go anywhere else.'

Schweitzer's pipe was not drawing very well. He knocked out the dead ash into a battered metal ashtray, then refilled it from his tobacco pouch.

'I get this tobacco sent from Paris,' he said, 'but it's sometimes an anxious wait for it to arrive.'

'I'm sure I could source some for you if you ever run low.'

'God forbid that I ever run out. It happened once, during my first time here. It was disastrous. I had to resort to cigarettes, but I could not get on with *them* at all.'

Schweitzer re-lit his pipe and was content again. He seemed to be a man of simple pleasures.

'I hope Helene can join me later,' he continued, in between puffs, 'when I am fully re-established here. She's already trained as a nurse, despite having never thought to take that road before.'

Such commitment, I thought. The Schweitzers were not people to flee back home with hopes in disarray and spirits quashed. This man had already made his mark, but he would go much further. I was sure of it.

'I do have an assistant now, though,' Schweitzer said, 'a countryman of yours, actually. Mr. Noel Gillespie, an Oxford man.'

This was news to me.

'Where is he?' I asked.

'He's gone up river on an errand for a few days.'

The conversation started to die again, and I realised Schweitzer was as tired as I was. We finished our tobacco and the doctor showed me to a bedroom. It was sparse but had a real bed in it, which was luxury indeed for me. Looking around at a few things, I thought this must be Gillespie's room.

It was one o'clock in the morning in Lambaréné, and I was lying in bed staring up at the ceiling. For me this meant another battle with sleep, and the dream it often brought. Not every night, but it was usually close by, lurking at the edge of my sanity, and all too often breaking through it. It was one of the reasons I came to Africa. I had thought that distance might bring relief, even closure, but that wish had proved forlorn.

The dream had many variations and cruel embellishments, but always at its core was the young German boy. He'd looked impossibly young for a soldier, more like fourteen than eighteen years old. Maybe he *had* been fourteen, for there were plenty of boy soldiers on all sides in that war. In the years since armistice he had become a permanent fixture in my mind. He had taken root there, the star of a demonic floor show designed just for me. Yes,

The Adam Hope Revue, more bloody and twisted than any Greek tragedy.

It had been a long day on the river and I felt my eyelids become heavy. They were eager to close, to shut down on life for a while. I tried to will myself an unbroken night's sleep, to link up with the constant thrum of night time insects, and sleep in sync with life here.

Above me, tiger moths were in action. They were cloth-like flying creatures, some almost the size of a man's hand. As they navigated their crazed way around the room I waved an ineffectual hand at the ones that came close, but they dodged it easily. Some dive-bombed the lantern, bouncing off it with singed or crushed wings. They were like miniature re-enactments of the aerial battles I used to watch from my Passchendaele trench.

I was envious of the freedom of our airmen at first, for they seemed so far away from the carnage, literally above it all. Then I watched as they began to drop to the ground in fiery thudding crashes, the immolated pilots still strapped in. They had no means of escape because they had no parachutes, but the Germans did, and the French, come to that.

The moths continued to circle, until they began to merge into the light of the lantern. As expected, at first I couldn't sleep. It never came easily to me these days. Even so, I was calmer tonight, and found the incessant drone of insects soothing rather than irritating. My eyelids became even heavier.

Messines Ridge, Flanders, July 1917. We've been trying to take it for three years, but always Fritz has pushed us back. A few hundred thousand men have died here, fighting over an eighty foot-high mound in the landscape. It's not much more than a hunk of raised mud now, but it's what lies beyond it that has fixated the top brass for a long time. It's just a railway, but a railway that is the main supply line of the German army.

I survived a long time as a Second lieutenant, and even longer as a First. I'm a captain now. Life expectancy here is often counted down in weeks for junior officers, but I've lasted since the first Somme offensive, when German Maxims ripped two thirds of my company apart. Lucky Hope they call me now.

Lucky Hope. I have grown to hate the name, for there is nothing lucky in staying alive in this hell. I've almost gotten used to seeing woods reduced to matchsticks, with perhaps a solitary tree still standing, like a crooked wooden finger pointing in accusation. And there's the blood, always blood. The gouged landscape is often reddened by it, and it has a supporting cast of torn bodies, mangled horses and ruined equipment. I see the orange muzzle flashes of a thousand heavy guns when an attack is imminent, hear the scream of whizz-bangs going overhead, and the cries and shrieks of the myriad wounded, and finally, smell the gut-churning stench of the dead.

Sometimes I want out so much I can taste the sweetness of death, and savour the release it might bring, but it's not enough to quell the fear I feel, that sinking in the pit of the stomach at the thought of the end. Fear is a very tricky customer. It's always there, but sometimes it rears up to grab you by the guts and starts to wrench them inside out. It is the thought of pain I fear more than death, that I will become part of the awful scenes I have witnessed. Men staring in dumbfounded disbelief at their missing arms and legs, until agony pushes through the shock and they start to scream.

The boredom is another killer, and almost as deadly as the fighting. It waits for me between each action, a slow drip of time as routines are carried out, just as sure to drag you down as the mud of any bomb crater. That's when that black dog of depression grips me in its jaw and starts to gnaw away. Each inactive day is like a small lifetime, and trench routine will be forever etched in my mind.

5am Stand To! As if we haven't been standing to all bloody night, but the army likes to draw a neat line under everything. Nights can never be for sleeping. Even when the guns have stopped they are for working — digging new trenches, getting supplies, planning ridiculous actions. Then come the dreaded nocturnal patrols, borderline suicide missions every one.

I remember my first patrol in the dark out there very well. Not that it's ever really dark at the front. Any sounds heard in no man's land are sure to attract a flare and a burst of gunfire, maybe even a shell or two, if it's a particularly bad night. I was a second lieutenant then, green as a cucumber, and still with enough jingoistic bullshit in me to invite a quick death. Our orders were to try to grab an unaware Fritz and haul him back to our lines for interrogation. It was standard practice on both sides, and a dangerous waste of time, in my opinion. Any intelligence gained never seemed to help us much. Usually we only learned the names of the German regiments in the opposing trenches.

There have been many such actions since, but it's that first one that remains so clear in my mind. It was a bitterly cold January night, and enthusiasm quickly turned to anxiety as I crawled out of the trench with a corporal and two men, all much more experienced than I was, and very much aware they were being led by a rookie officer not long out of school.

There were so many things lying out in the pockmarked, gouged-out spaces of the killing fields that could betray your presence. Clanking against abandoned ordnance was the worst, for just the scrape of a boot against metal was enough to alert the very good German snipers. They were only about eight hundred yards away, and we were crawling closer all the time.

Crawling was the operative word. We moved on our bellies over the muddy slime, trying to avoid the festering corpses of the unknown dead. Corporal Wilson let out an audible curse as one of his hands sank into the rotting guts of someone who might once have been a comrade, or the enemy, who knows, but nothing happened, apart from a rat scurrying away.

We knew there would be an outlying observation post, and that was our target. Somewhere out here a German patrol was doing the same as us. Occasionally two such patrols met and there was a sharp firefight, leaving a few wounded survivors to inch their bloody way back to their lines, where they could die amongst their own.

We had identified a target, and were close to it.

'They usually only have two blokes in them observation posts, sir,' my corporal whispered. 'One to keep a look out and one to have a bloody good kip. With a bit of luck we can surprise the buggers before there's any shooting.'

They were the last words Wilson ever uttered. A shot rang out. It was close because I saw the muzzle flash of the rifle. Wilson got it through the neck. Blood pumped from in it a thin red waterfall, and most of it pumped over me. It was lucky that the German patrol was not officer led, because a Luger pistol is much better in the dark than a cumbersome Mauser.

Three of the enemy appeared out of the gloom and I shot wildly at them, but a few rounds hit home. A man behind me, still prone in the dirt, shot another with his rifle, and the third faded back into the darkness very quickly. Not that it was dark for very long. All manners of stuff opened up, small arms of every description, and they were all firing at us.

We joined Wilson, lying flat in the dirt in the hope that we wouldn't be hit. Wilson died without saying a word as I took his identification tag and closed his staring eyes.

We made our way back. If there was a record for rapid crawling we must have broken it. I could feel the whine of bullets going past, but if there was no flare we had a chance. Our men were returning fire now, shooting aimlessly at any flashes they saw. It took us a long fifteen minutes, but the three of us got back in one piece.

I felt my gorge rising the whole way. Wilson's blood had seeped through my tunic in a sticky mess as I tensed for something to hit me, hoping it would be fatal and instant. I was so grateful to be pulled back down into our own trench by the rough hands of squaddies. I had lots of pats on the back, and a chorus of 'You're okay now, sir.'

Barely conscious, I just about held it together in front of my men, then went to report my failure to my commanding officer. Captain Carter seemed quite surprised that I had got back alive, and offered me a whisky, a small one.

'It's a shame about Corporal Wilson,' he said, 'but it's all good experience for you, Hope, and you'll be all the better for it. Do you know, I think you're going to be a lucky young bugger.'

So I was dubbed Lucky Hope and I haven't even been wounded since then. The closest I've come was having an epaulette shot off. A young corporal crouching next to me at the time had thought that funny, until a second rifle round hit him dead centre of the forehead, giving him a third metal eye and a puzzled look on his face as he sank down into the mud. I can't even remember his name now. Was it Daniels, Davies? Something with a D, I think.

Our July attack on the ridge surprises the enemy, and is successful, for a while. *For a while* could serve as an epitaph for the whole damn Flanders campaign, hopeless and insanely brave cut-and-thrusts by both sides that ultimately got nowhere.

Ah, here comes the young German boy. His timing is impeccable, as always in my dream. He sits up in front of me quickly, the top of his head spilling blood and brains. Where the top of his head used to be. And he is smiling.

It happens when we are pushing the Germans from their trenches and dugouts; hand-to-hand fighting is taking place all along the line. I have my Colt 45 in my hand, a Yank gun that I have bought myself. A lot of officers use them because we don't trust the regulation Webley, which doesn't like the mud and wet. The Colt is a beast, a lump of iron impervious to all weathers. Men are charging all around me, their bayonets looking for soft flesh. The force of our attack has overwhelmed our enemy and we are pressing it home.

The boy must have been hiding in the dug out, too terrified to run or to fight. Maybe it is the sight of an officer that draws him out, hands above his head, shouting *Kamerad* as he comes towards me. I have time to think, so there's no excuse, but I still shoot. I am so tired, so desperately tired. The fear of death clashes with the irresistible adrenalin of action, and the need for it all to be over.

So I shoot, the heavy Colt kicking in my hand as it releases its charge. My aim is poor but fatal. The top of the boy's head is gone and I see his eyes for the first time: so clear, so blue. The boy, for I can see how young he is, sinks down on his knees quite slowly, as if he's in prayer. He tries to say something, I think it's *Kamerad* again, but I'm his killer, not his comrade. I'm clapped on the back by one of the men coming up behind me.

'You dun for that bastard, sir,' the man shouts, as he plunges onwards with bayoneted rifle. I plunge on too.

The boy is getting up off his knees now. He's coming towards me, his arms stretched out wide in appeal. He's just inches away from me and I can see my awful reflection in his clear blue eyes. It's awful because his killer is a vision of horror, his face filthy with fuzzy stubble, sweat and trench mud, an apparition from hell if ever there was one. The boy is trying to touch me, perhaps he wants to take me with him, take me down, take me down...

*

I sat up quickly, grabbing at air with my hands, and desperately pushing the mosquito net away. At first I thought I was trapped, like a wild animal caught in a net.

My right hand collided with a moth, making me shout out. It was the boy, and I was touching the soft pulp of his ruined head, until I realised I was awake again. For a moment I didn't know where I was, so vivid was the wartime nightmare.

Of course. I was at Lambaréné, the guest of a man of God, a man of peace and learning, a man of music. Something large scuttled under my camp bed, but this was a land of scuttling things. Best not to worry about them overmuch, for they'd still be here long after I was gone. It was probably a rat on night manoeuvres.

I tried to rest easy, sinking back on the hard bed, my body soaked through with sweat. There was the usual drift of jungle noise outside. Night birds crazed with song merged with the solid drone of insect battalions, but I could still hear the sluggish movement of the Ogowe. It seemed to suck at the bank as it passed by.

I thought of Laura again, for the second time that night. I had tried to blot her out, but am still not quite able to do so. The strange thing is I never dream about her, but she's in my waking thoughts, if they are waking thoughts. Sometimes I'm not really sure if I am asleep or not. At times like this I seem to exist in a kind of no man's land between waking and sleep.

It is springtime back home and I can almost taste the fresh breeze, and see the hillsides being peppered with green again. Home was a safe place, and sometimes I long for it almost as much as I long for a drink. They say time is a great healer, but that's such a lie. For me, the farther away memories become in time, the sharper they seem. They loom out of the past to catch you unawares, and the raw ones never do heal.

I managed a few more snatches of sleep, but was up at first light to check on the men. I was in time to see a hazy sun rise over the jungle. This was the best time of day for me, when all the noises of the night died down before the day shift began. There seemed to be a quiet truce for a short while. The sun was kinder too, almost soothing before it took on its punishing strength.

A hut had been found for Julius and four others to sleep in, and my NCO was emerging sleepily from its entrance, rubbing at his already glistening black chest. He was an imposing figure, a few inches taller than my own six feet, with an athletic yet muscular body, a far cry from the small Tommies I used to command in the war. That was when I looked poverty full in its rotten eyes for the first time, as most of the officers were so much taller than their men. That was why they died so quickly, their height attracted the attention of German snipers.

All through my childhood poverty had been a distant thing, read about but never experienced, something that afflicted the great unwashed, as my father put it, and was entirely their fault. I was an only child living with a hard-drinking, controlling father, and a self-effacing mother. We lived in a grand house much too large for three, in a leafy location a few miles outside Cardiff. I'd always seen myself as Welsh, as I'd been born in Cardiff to an English father and Welsh mother, but this annoyed and even enraged the old man.

'It's holding you back, boy!' he used to roar at me. 'Forget about this bloody country. Forget about its bloody language. This place is good for just three things, coal, steel and money, and language and poetry don't make money.' Or, 'If ever the coal and steel run out, this place will be good for nothing but cripples and drunks, and I didn't sink a fortune in school fees for you to end up as a cripple or drunk. You're British, boy — *British* — and I don't want you to forget it!'

I never did forget it — his words anyway.

Hope Senior ran a profitable coal export company, and my education had hardly cost him a fortune. Luckily for me, my father had baulked at the fees of the major English public schools, even though he could well afford them. He enrolled me in a barely adequate private school in Cardiff. I did well enough there, though, and was on course for Oxford until 1914 got in the way.

Julius brought me out of my thoughts. He must have gotten used to me going into brown studies by now. He probably thought I was a little bit cracked, like all white men, but as we were in the midst of lepers my mood concerned him a bit more than usual.

'Boss all good?' he asked. 'All good with boss? No bad spirits?'

'All good.'

My host was already active. Arrangements for my men to eat had been made, which perked them up no end. They trudged off, led by the stumps-for-hands man. I went back to join Schweitzer.

'We have our first surgery at eight,' Schweitzer told me, as he met me on the rickety wooden veranda. 'We like to start before the heat becomes too oppressive. I'm afraid you will have to breakfast alone, Mr. Hope, but Joseph will attend to you.'

Joseph served me a breakfast of bread, honey and coffee that actually tasted like coffee, not like the ersatz rubbish I usually had to endure. When I'd finished I went back out onto the veranda, to see Julius and the others lolling in the shade of a hut. Julius walked up to me in that languid gait of his, as if each leg followed the other with reluctance.

'Boys like it here now, boss,' he said. 'They have food without work.'

'No more evil spirits?'

'Oganga watch over us. He strong god.'

'Well, don't get too used to it,' I said, 'we won't be here long.'

The wet season was imminent. When it came, heavy skies would empty for a few weeks, replenishing the forest. As if in step with my thoughts, the first rain started to fall, light at first, then quickly increasing, until solid grey sheets of water began to soak the forest trees.

'Doesn't it come down so,' Schweitzer said, as he joined me a while later.

I nodded agreement.

'But this weather is good for our surgery,' the doctor said. 'More people come in the rainy season, because it's easier for them to stop working. This is just the rain's first skirmish. Next week it will start in earnest.'

'Don't I know it. Are you getting anywhere?' I asked, 'medically, that is?'

'If you mean am I helping people, yes. Simple preventive medicine can do wonders, but disease here is reinforced by ignorance and poverty. The one feeds off the other.'

'Is there a cure for those — anywhere?'

'I see you have a liberal dose of scepticism, Mr. Hope. So many people do. Maybe you'd like to join me on my rounds, now that surgery is over?'

I was not keen to do so, but had not lost sight of common courtesy. I followed the doctor to the huts. I had seen lepers before, but only singly. It took me a moment for my eyes to adjust to the diminished light, and then they appeared. Six figures were sitting in a row, and six sets of eyes looked up hopefully as we entered, hopefully at Schweitzer, not at me. When I looked at them, as kindly as I could muster, they cast their eyes down again, in shame, or fear of the stranger, as lepers had done for thousands of years.

A woman of indeterminate age reached up a hand to clasp one of Schweitzer's. At least it had been a hand. Now it was a clump of knotted flesh, fingers fused together into a solid mass, much like the man who had first greeted us here. At least her face was not affected yet, apart from its complexity of lines and wrinkles, but the man next to her looked barely human. His nose had been eaten away and his face was covered in hard, lumpy nodules.

I remembered a childhood trip to Ireland, marvelling at the Giant's Causeway on the coast of Antrim. This poor man's face was like a miniature version of it, but instead of stone pillars, his were made of flesh moulded into a human tragedy. His deep-set eyes were almost submerged in his ruined face. They cowered there, as if ashamed to be part of this awful display.

Schweitzer touched my arm gently.

'Rather sobering, isn't it, Mr. Hope?'

'Yes, it is rather.'

'Don't worry, no one here knows any English, just a smattering of French to go with their native dialect.'

Giant's Causeway Man was trying to smile, but he couldn't quite manage it. His eyes were like two chips of glass trapped in a gruesome cage. He too reached out a hand, or rather a piece of flesh moulded into a dull point. I took it, though I wanted to shrink away. His hand felt like it had been carved from wood, so thickened was it with flesh that had been so cruelly re-arranged.

'I see you are a man of some substance,' Schweitzer said. 'Apart from my assistant no other white man has ever done that here. People still hold mediaeval views, you see, Biblical views indeed. *Lepra* is the ancient Greek word for outcast.'

'Yes, I did know that.'

'Ah, you are educated in the classics, but are you educated in leprosy? You did know that it's not contagious?'

'I wasn't sure.'

'I thought that was the case. As I say, a man of substance.'

Schweitzer ushered me onwards, pointing out various aspects of the hospital. If any place could be ramshackle but ordered at the same time, it was Lambaréné. Schweitzer was a bit like that too. His hair was never really under control, but his clothes were very neat. He looked like a bookish man about to talk a stroll around Montmartre. Missionary types usually irritated me. Africa had not asked for their concern, and many of them could not withstand the rigours of the life here, and soon left, but Schweitzer was different.

*

Word came upriver that my steamer had been fixed. It would be at Lambaréné in a few days, and Pieters was bringing it up personally. I was given a note saying he'd like a change of scene but this really meant he wanted to be paid immediately. The Belgian always thought that one day I would disappear into the interior for good, owing him money.

Pieters was the last person I wanted to see at Lambaréné, and I prayed that he would at least be partly sober, and that my merchandise was safe. Pieters would be disappointed regarding my debt to him, though. He would have to wait for the second half of it until I started trading again.

There was mainly low-grade rum on board this time, which was easier to get than whisky. I used it to barter with the locals in exchange for timber. Timber was the true god here, the most powerful *oganga*. Mahogany and ebony made good prices, and when I couldn't get that there was always *okoumé*, which grew in abundance here and was good for plywood. I had all bases covered, hardwood for the European furniture market, and plywood for mass use.

I played the logging companies on one hand, and the chiefs of the interior on the other. It was a lucrative business, but it made me a renegade to my own, and a white devil to some of the people along the river, mainly the ones who couldn't get hold of my rum. I relied on greed, the greed of tribal headmen and European businessmen, and it had worked well for me. It was a trade that I had fallen into all too easily. I was not proud of it, nor was not ashamed of it.

Pieters arrived when he said he would, which was quite unusual for him. The *River Ghost* came around a bend in the river in a wide loop to avoid the shallows, and announced its presence with would-be blasts of its hooter, but it was really more a series of beeps than blasts. The noise scattered the river birds, and they rose up in a squawking, complaining mass of wings. It also roused a few of Schweitzer's patients who were snoozing in the sun. They sat up quickly with startled looks on their faces, but then smiled as they saw the steamboat approaching.

Schweitzer walked down to the riverbank with me to greet the boat, accompanied by most of Lambaréné, it seemed. The arrival of a steamboat was a big deal here.

There was lots of excited chatter as the *River Ghost* moored up in the deepest part of the river, and animated locals quickly surrounded it in a variety of tiny vessels. As a dugout conveyed him to the shore, Pieters stood upright on it unsteadily and waved. The Belgian always needed discreet handling, because I had seen him erupt many times over the smallest thing. He'd laid out more than a few men in his time here, white and black.

Pieters jumped onto the sandy banking and stuck out a gnarled hand.

'*Goeije morn*,' Pieters yelled.

'I suppose that means good morning, but you know I don't know any Flemish.'

'Then you should learn some, man.'

I could smell rum on him, my rum, but Pieters was not noticeably intoxicated, which was a relief.

'How was the trip up?' I asked.

'Nice and smooth, *ja*, nice and smooth. I've got that old engine running as sweet as a nut for you.'

Pieters turned towards Schweitzer.

'Ah, the good doctor. I haven't seen you since you left Cape Lopez.'

Pieters gave Schweitzer a mock salute.

'You are welcome, Mr. Pieters.' Schweitzer followed up with something in French, causing Pieters to shrug his shoulders.

'No French, Doc, I've told you that before. Flemish and what Hope here calls my twisted English. I have a few parcels on board for you. Papers and stuff. Oh, and a large chest. The men will bring that ashore now.'

Schweitzer's face lit up like a young boy expecting gifts.

'Ah, my manuscripts have arrived at last. Come up to the house, Mr. Pieters, to refresh yourself.'

'I'll join you later,' I said. 'I want to check over my steamer first.'

Pieters burst out with laughter.

'Hah, check that all your goods are still there, more like.'

Pieters had an amazing display of teeth. Some healthy, some rotten, some missing and all deeply stained by nicotine. Julius and another man had joined us. Julius glared at the

Belgian. He had never liked Pieters. Not many people did like him. I wasn't sure that I liked him myself.

Pieters walked up the slope with Schweitzer, putting an over-familiar arm on his shoulder. Like many whites on the coast, Pieters did not understand the doctor's presence here. He thought the hospital was a crazy thing for a white man to be doing, for there was no profit in it.

I found the *River Ghost was* in good order. Pieters had even polished its nameplate, the gold lettering of *River Ghost* standing out proudly against its worn wooden background. It was a ridiculous name for a ponderous river barge but I hadn't thought to change it, because that would mean too much form-filling with the French authorities. That lot had a form for everything.

I planned to set off the next morning. The first rain had not lasted long and we were due for maybe a week of fresh days before the wet season really set in. This was time I had to use well.

Valuable trading time had been lost, so Pieters would have to come along. I did not have the time to take him back to the coast. He would not like it but I hadn't paid him yet, and that would keep him onboard, in more ways than one.

We spent an awkward night with the doctor, awkward because Pieters made no secret of the fact that he longed for a drink, and none was available. If I'd let him he would have gone back out to the *Ghost* to replenish his thirst, but that was never going to happen. To shut him up, and to keep him out of Schweitzer's hair, I promised him a half case of rum as a bonus on top of his fee.

When Schweitzer finished his day's work he joined us for dinner, and even Pieters was impressed with the food Joseph served.

'Better than the swill I get at the docks,' he said, trying to whisper, but Pieters' whispering was another man's raised voice.

'You should be proud you have such engineering skill, Mr. Pieters,' Schweitzer said, as we formed our own after-dinner smoking club. 'It is good for a man to work with his hands.'

Pieters shrugged, and lit another of my cheap cigars, trying to form a ring with the smoke he exhaled, his lips pursed in the attempt. He'd been trying to do this for years without success.

'I pride myself on some skill with organs,' Schweitzer said, 'but I don't mean the human kind. I'm talking about church organs. I took one apart once, in my local church back home. It was ailing, and it was a good feeling to restore it to health.'

'How about a few tunes on that, then?' Pieters said, interrupting Schweitzer as he nodded towards the piano.

'I don't think the doctor plays *tunes*,' I murmured.

'How about a little Bach?' Schweitzer said, seemingly unruffled by Pieters' rudeness.

I thought how unusual it would be, listening to a Bach fugue, thousands of miles away from what is laughingly called civilization. I knew that Schweitzer was a celebrated organist in Europe, but I soon realised his piano playing was also very good.

The doctor was calm as he lost himself in his music, and his carefully measured playing went well with the

Lambaréné night. It blended in with the thrum of insects and the faint sound of the Ogowe drifting past the camp. I wondered how many of his patients could hear the piano as it carried through the open windows, and what on earth they might make of it. I had a rather thin knowledge of classical music, but I could recognize a master at work in any profession.

Pieters continued to smoke, but he too became quiet as he looked out into the night. His fingers tapped along in time with the music as he continued his endless quest for the perfect smoke ring.

Schweitzer played with his eyes closed for most of the time. It was as if Bach was in the room with him. He played for about twenty minutes and then excused himself early.

'This is a rare late night for me,' he said. 'No doubt I shall pay a price for it when I get up at six-thirty in the morning. Gentleman, please stay up as long as you want. You are my guests.'

We bid our host good night, and I was left to set out my plans for the next few weeks. Unfortunately Pieters had to be part of them.

'You can't expect me to take you back to the Cape and then track all the way back up here,' I said. 'That would be a waste of time and money.'

'Yeah, *your* time and *your* money.' Pieters said. 'And speaking of money, where the hell is mine?'

Pieters wanted to unleash an angry outburst at me, but he thought better of it. He was a bulky man, and handy with his fists, but he knew I was much handier. That was thanks to Tom Stevens, one of my company sergeants. He had given me many impromptu boxing lessons in the rare times the regiment had been relieved and sent to the rear. Stevens had been British middleweight champion before the war, and it seemed to amuse him that an officer wanted to learn to box.

'Well, where is it, then?' Pieters said. 'The money for that new screw and all the other stuff?'

'You'll get it. You know you always do, but with the steamer being out of action, cash flow is a bit stressed at the moment. Once I sell the next shipment of timber I'll be up and running again.'

'I knew it. You're bloody broke, man. The great white Hope — I don't think.'

Pieters was almost right, but I always kept an emergency fund in a French colonial bank.

'I have money to collect up river.' I said. 'Do you remember that American missionary, Collins?'

'Yeah, I remember him. Tall, bony guy. I gave him a year out here at best when I saw him on the docks. He brought his wife with him too.'

'Yes he did, and he's done two years now, so maybe he's a stayer. He owes me money for the last lot of stuff I brought up for him.'

'You mean you *hope* you'll get paid. The last person I'd trust with money is a God-Squadder.'

'Pieters, your cynicism never fails to disappoint me.'

'It's never disappointed me either.'

'Collins is good for it. He's always paid before. Collins has a good supply line with his people. He's a lot better off than Schweitzer is here, I think.'

'Well, that wouldn't be hard. Look at this place. It's more like a shanty town than a hospital.'

'Keep your voice down. Look, why don't you get back onboard the *Ghost*?' I said. 'Tell you what, you can fill yourself up with a bottle of rum — on me. But if you do, remember we'll be casting off at first light.'

The Belgian looked at me suspiciously.

'Don't fancy sharing a room with me eh?'

'Who the hell would?'

Pieters laughed.

'Well, you got that right, English. Okay, get a few of your men to take me over to the *River Ghost*, magnificently repaired by me, Jan Pieters. And don't wake me up in the morning. There's no need to, because *I'm* not one of your men.'

'Okay, and Pieters?'

'Yeah?'

'You know I'm not English.'

Pieters shrugged and waved me a lazy farewell.

'What the hell does it matter?' he muttered.

I had to first find the hut Julius was sleeping in, and then rouse him, which always took time. He offered me a few complaining looks, but roughly pulled up another man to help, and they took Pieters across the Ogowe to the *Ghost*.

I watched them disappear into the gloom, and for one devious yet glorious moment, I imagined a nocturnal hippo tipping them up. My men were excellent swimmers, but I knew Pieters, despite his knowledge of boats, was a true landlubber who couldn't manage a stroke. His demise would help solve my financial woes in one watery descent.

Schweitzer would be appalled at such a thought, and deep down, so was I.

I turned in myself, to the simple bedroom Schweitzer had provided. Maybe I could get a good night's sleep tonight, but I sat up in the bed for a while and stared at the ceiling, enclosed in an imperfect mosquito net. I realised I had been out here for almost four years now.

Gabon had provided two things Europe wanted in the last three hundred years or so, which was timber and people. People in the form of slaves. This had been one of the most fertile parts of Africa for the slave trade, until the British and French finally ended it.

The French had tried to establish potatoes, rice and even wheat in Gabon, but the African soil had rejected all of them. The only notable success was the cattle that had been introduced to the pastures of the interior, where they thrived. So that left just the timber, for me and the other traders on the river.

The French had a better record in Gabon than other powers in Africa, but that wasn't saying much. The Germans took a harder line, the Belgians had brutalised the Congo, and the Portuguese were even worse further south, I'd been told.

Before I settled on Gabon I had taken time to travel down the west coast of Africa, and had seen the results of white rule everywhere. It was relentless as much as ruthless. Maybe if I'd come out before the war I would have been less sensitive to it, but my wartime experiences had put paid to all that. The war had instilled a sense of injustice in me, despite the work I was engaged in.

It had been so difficult to establish myself here in the early days. I almost thought of abandoning my plan and going home with my tail between my legs, probably to immerse myself in the drudgery of a safe commercial job. Use your commission and war record, a senior officer once told me, and you'll get a comfortable billet. Yes, maybe I would, and the soulless existence that went with it, each day wasted doing work that did not interest me. Add an ill-judged marriage and my life might become a prison. So I'd stuck at it on the Ogowe, until I gained a foothold as a trader.

I pulled the mosquito net tighter around me as I heard their high-pitched whines coming close. Usually when you did hear them it was too late, for they had struck, but this night I slept soundly for once, almost as soon as my head hit the hard pillow.

I woke at sun-up the next morning, just as the dawn chorus was getting going. Broadbills, wagtails, and an assortment of wildfowl were all limbering up, plus many other birds whose names I didn't yet know. This country was rich and diverse in its wildlife, and never more so than at break of day.

As I thought, Pieters did not join me for breakfast. He would be sleeping it off in one of the *Ghost's* bunks, and I hoped it wasn't mine. His behaviour in the presence of Schweitzer had been embarrassing, but I knew that if Pieters sensed my disapproval, he'd act up all the more. I wondered if his past tormented him as much as mine. He told me once that he'd 'had to get out of Belgium fast,' but had not elaborated. He'd probably left a woman and maybe children behind him, and definitely a few crimes.

Schweitzer was about to leave for his surgery when I joined him.

'Ah, good morning, Mr. Hope. I'm told Mr. Pieters continued his evening on your steamer.'

'He certainly did, Doctor.'

'The need for alcohol that so many whites here have saddens me.'

'Maybe it's the climate.'

'Perhaps so, but I think it's also the loneliness. I meet so many who seem to be running away from their former lives. Distant countries have always been good for that, haven't they?'

'I doubt very much that you are one of them, Dr. Schweitzer.'

'No, I'm not. I came to Africa running *towards* something, Mr. Hope. My destiny is here, at Lambaréné.'

'Yes, I can see that.'

'I think you see rather a lot. Joseph has prepared breakfast for you, by the way.'

'Thank you. Oh, did you get the coffee? There were a few packs in the goods my men unloaded for you.'

'I certainly did. It is excellent, and there is a pot of it waiting for you.'

'Thank you.'

'I was thinking earlier that you must have built up an excellent knowledge of the hardwoods here,' Schweitzer said.

'Hardly excellent, but I do know the good stuff, and what's best to buy.'

'Indeed. The reason I ask is that I've become quite knowledgeable about the timber here myself.'

'Really?'

'Yes. I thought, as it's the main export of Gabon, I should get to know more about it.'

'I see.'

I was beginning to wonder if there was anything that Schweitzer *didn't* know about. Talking to some of the colonials on the coast it seemed that the man had qualifications as long as your arm. I'd met a few men like him in the army. It seemed like they had forty-eight hours in their day, such was their industry.

'Perhaps we can discuss this further when you next visit us,' Schweitzer said.

'Yes, I'd like that.'

Schweitzer thrust out a hand, quite abruptly.

'I won't be able to see you off. It's another very busy working day for me, so I'll bid you farewell now.'

I accepted his hand.

'You told me last night that you are going upriver?' Schweitzer said.

'Yes, for few days.'

'Then perhaps you could stop at Lambaréné on your way back?'

'Yes, I could, but Pieters will still be with me.'

'That is not a problem. He barks a lot, but I doubt there is much bite to the man. Will you be bringing timber down with you?'

'Yes, we'll be towing the smaller teak logs down on a barge. Musbewi's men will raft the big stuff down after the rains come.'

'Ay yes, the *okoumé* logs. I like to call that *faux teak*.'

'That's a good name for it. False teak indeed. I was fooled myself once, when I first started trading.'

Schweitzer almost laughed, but made do with a broad smile. It was the first time I'd seen him do so. It lit up his face and for one brief moment he became a different man, and the cares that weighed so heavily on his shoulders seemed to disappear.

'Yes, the natives here can be a cunning lot,' Schweitzer said.

I felt a little uncomfortable to hear Schweitzer describe the locals like this. People would have been more appropriate, but Schweitzer was much older than I was. He was very much a Victorian, and his relationship with Africa might be less complicated than mine. I returned the doctor's smile.

'Thank you for the hospitality, Doctor.'

'Not at all, Mr. Hope. You are very welcome.'

Now that we had broken bread, as it were, I looked forward to talking to Schweitzer again, and when the time was right I hoped to spend a longer spell at Lambaréné. I planned to make a substantial donation, when I could, because I knew the doctor's funds were always meagre. This was even more reason to get cracking with business.

Breakfast over and my thoughts gathered, I watched from the shoreline as Julius got the sleepy men ready to leave. Their initial fear of stopping here was now replaced by sadness at the thought of going, for they had been fed well, and that was no small thing this far into the heart of the country.

Emotions on the river changed as quickly as the weather. Sun-baked anger could replace the torpor of the dank jungle in seconds. Sometimes it led to violence, as old feuds surfaced between the men of different tribes. There was also a long history of cannibalism here, and some said it had not yet died out.

I looked in on Pieters when I got back aboard the *River Ghost*. He was snoring loudly in his bunk, and was soaked through with rum-infused night sweat. It glistened on him like fresh rain. I thought it wise to let him sleep it off, and it was better that he stayed out of my way, for the boat was becoming a little crowded. I had the three-man crew Pieters had brought up with him, plus my own five, and they would all want paying.

Once on board, Julius reverted to his main job of chief engineer — well, he was my *only* engineer. He proudly put on the third-hand British naval jacket I had provided for him. It was his pride and joy, and you could sense the man's confidence surge as he wore it. He lusted after a matching hat too, but I hadn't yet been able to provide him with one.

I sent Julius below to carry out the checks I had taught him, and Pieters was not around to bark instructions, threats and insults in his ear. Julius was not sure how the engine really worked, but he knew all the components and how to look after them.

Becoming captain of a steamboat had also been a steep learning curve for me. Watching the boats that used to fetch up at the bustling Cardiff docks was my only prior experience of anything nautical, and of no real use at all.

Once I had bought the *River Ghost*, I paid Pieters to give me a crash course in all things riverboat, and to my surprise I took to it quite well. At least I could thank the army for that, or at least the enlisted men, because I learned a lot about practicality from them in that war. Now I knew how to use my hands to good purpose. My parents would have been horrified at the thought of me doing manual labour.

Buying the *River Ghost* had taken most of my inheritance. My father died just after Armistice Day. He went out with his boots on, keeling over his desk as he returned to the office, after what would have certainly been a liquid lunch. His heart had called time on him.

My last letter to my mother, sent on the twelfth of November 1918, told her that I had survived the war. Her returning letter to me told me that my father was dead. There would have been very little chance I could have got home in time for the funeral, even if I had wanted to, so I never even mentioned it to my commanding officer.

The war had gone on for an eternity, and you could only fear death for so long. After that it was just a short dangerous step to welcoming it, such was the unbearable fatigue and ennui between combat. I had survived nearly four years on active duty, and the last two years had been like that for me. But I was still alive, which almost made me unique. A miracle officer indeed.

It had been a cramped, cold and smoky trip back to Wales. I came across the Channel in a packet boat bursting with troops in the same state as I was. An angry, slate-grey sea tossed the boat around, and many were sick, despairingly heaving over the side into the dark night. It seemed like a final indignity for them.

I did not stop long in London, despite the exhortations of my fellow officers. I took a rattling train down from Paddington to Cardiff. It was a cold and grey winter's day but the countryside still looked wonderful. There were no destroyed landscapes, decimated woods, or large expanses of land turned to mud. My uniform drew a few admiring glances from young women, but I knew that wouldn't last. Once the novelty wore off I would become a period piece, a memory of a conflict that everyone wanted to forget.

When I did finally get back to Wales it was a strange homecoming. I had hoped that being free of my father might have given mother a new lease of life. She was still not fifty years old, but there seemed a permanent tiredness about her. It seemed to be woven into her very soul. I could sense this, for most of us who had served felt the same. I think she had served in her own war, a much longer one than mine, and had given up on life a long time ago.

'You are home then,' was all my mother said when I walked through the front door. She touched me lightly on the shoulder, but took back her hand quickly to fuss with her hair.

At least I was coming back to an inheritance. Most of the enlisted men returning were faced with disinterested ex-employers telling them that things had moved on, and moved on without them. Homes fit for heroes proved to be yet another lie.

I soon put away my uniform for good, then spent some uncomfortable weeks with my mother, until my father's affairs were settled. I thought his death might have changed things between us, but it was not to be. By the time I left I think we both realised that we had very little to say to each other.

I went below with Julius to check the coal bunker, to reassure myself we had enough fuel to steam about fifty miles further upriver, and then get back down to Cape Lopez. We did have enough, and it looked pretty decent Welsh steam coal. It was a huge improvement on the wood that had once fuelled steamers. I pressed a few of the smaller lumps with my hands and enjoyed getting them dirty. For a moment I experienced a touch of nostalgia, but it was false, for my life was even further removed from that of a Welsh miner than it was from the men that manned the *River Ghost*.

Julius shouted at his boys to get shovelling fuel into the burners, revelling in his authority. He made a point of staring at the boiler gauges, tapping them and glancing at me for approval. I nodded it. Julius knew that if the gauges reached a certain point he had to come to get me very quickly, no matter what time of day or night it was. The *River Ghost* had already lost one screw, but an exploding water boiler would be an even greater disaster. It had been known to happen in the old paddleboat days, but things had improved and become safer since then.

I left Julius to get on with it, and went back up on deck to greet the morning sun. It was flooding the bridge with light, and old wooden fittings gleamed with a yellow sheen. It was a good moment.

Julius wiped sweat from his eyes as Hope left. Last year, when he was granted a week's leave, he'd found a French book in Cape Lopez that dealt with boats like the *River Ghost*. It became his secret for the next six months. Its contents tested him, but he kept at it, using the French dictionary his family had given him when he left his village. His father had bartered for it from Father Pierre. He was the French priest who had taught Julius at his village school, when he could spare the time to go there, for often work had to come first.

Julius' father could not read a word in any language, none of his large family could, but he told his son that books might be the future, so he should learn from them well. His father, and everyone that had come before him, relied on an oral history and literature, handed down from generation to generation, taking on weight as time accumulated.

Julius had learned first hand the complicated story of his country's past, sitting at his father's feet with his brothers and sisters. He heard about the slave traders who came, and how close his grandparents had came to being taken. He also learned that many of his people colluded with them. Those thought undesirable, or men captured in conflicts, were often sold to the white slavers. This made him sad but his father just shrugged when questioned about it, sometimes adding that 'people are people.'

Julius was sometimes enraged by the passiveness of his father, but the longer he worked with the whites the more he understood it. In his early working days, when he'd first come down to the coast, the French had used him as a beast of burden. He was tall and well built, so that marked him out as a useful manual worker, one that ate less than a horse or a donkey. He'd kept the fact that he was literate to himself, though sometimes a few of his fellow workers in the docks saw him with a book and were astounded.

Julius had to tread carefully even with Hope. The boss was the best white man he had worked with, and on a good day, Julius felt he was being treated as an equal. On a good day. He longed to tell Hope that he could read, and understood the boat's engines much better than the captain realised, but always caution stayed his hand. His pay on the riverboat was the best he'd earned, and sometimes there was enough left to take home to his family, much to the delight of his mother.

*

Schweitzer took a short break from his early morning surgery to watch the *River Ghost* depart. He dried his hands on an old towel as he saw a thin plume of smoke rise up from the boat's funnel. He was reminded of the steam engines of his childhood, and how he liked to watch those smoking giants thunder past on the local railway lines. That was before music and faith had taken hold of him, and his serious studies had begun. Schweitzer sometimes wondered if he had become old before his time. He had ceased to join in the games of his friends at too young an age, especially the ones who liked to kill wild birds. Before he was very old a new lifestyle was forming, many strands of it coming together to shape his worldview, and the man he was to become.

The steamboat gave a sharp burst on its whistle as it began to negotiate the first bend of the river. It brought up clouds of wading birds as it did so. As the *River Ghost* faded into the morning haze Schweitzer gave a small wave of farewell, though he knew he could not possibly be seen from the boat.

Schweitzer imagined Adam Hope standing on the deck, a capable man in charge of his watery world. This young man intrigued him. He sensed there was something different about him. Hope shared some of the characteristics that many Europeans had here. He had the same restlessness, the moodiness and the fugitive air of someone looking over his shoulder at his past, as if it might catch him up at any time. Maybe it was the sins of his past.

Hope showed all those traits, but Schweitzer sensed other qualities in the man. He had not shied away from the lepers, even though he hadn't known the disease could not be transmitted by touch. That took courage. Constant exposure to such things as nasal droplets was needed if leprosy was to transfer from person to person, but Hope had not known this. Schweitzer certainly did, for his own safety depended on it, and that of his small staff.

The need to take great care was the first thing Schweitzer had impressed on young Gillespie, who was a recent arrival at Lambaréné. Gillespie was to be his assistant for a while, and Schweitzer was glad to have him. He was impressed that Gillespie had taken a break from his Oxford studies to join him here. This young man would make a fine doctor one day, and he also shared the religious commitment that was needed at Lambaréné.

Gillespie had proved himself very quickly, arriving as he did in the midst of a dysentery outbreak. What a baptism of fire that was for the man. He was also good with the people here. He had a quiet nature; firm but kind seemed to be Gillespie's motto. Schweitzer liked that.

Gillespie's arrival had made things easier for Schweitzer to begin the rebuilding of the hospital. Even so, he wished that his wife were with him. Despite his workload, there was always time to think of her, and how he missed her quiet support. From the first time they had met Helene had been the calm in every storm he had encountered, but she could not be with him at Lambaréné this time, not yet. The conditions were too harsh, and they had a daughter now, Rhena. It seemed that he had barely seen her, and not being there to share her early journey in life hurt.

Lost in his thoughts, Schweitzer felt the loneliness of his missionary calling. Pointing it out in others did not mean he was immune to it himself. He pulled at his thick moustache with his fingers, a habit of his when he was deep in thought. The endless work at Lambaréné kept him constantly busy, but with Gillespie away, his isolation was enhanced.

The Great War, as they now called it, had brought his initial work here to a halt, and in those years of internment, time and neglect had eroded most of what he had done before. It was a daunting task to get it all back up and running again. Sometimes he felt like he was another Sisyphus, and Lambaréné was the rock that he constantly pushed up the hill, only to have it rolled back down by the gods every time. But with God's help, he would succeed here and Helene could indeed join him.

Joseph came to look for Schweitzer. The next patient had been readied for an amputation. His arm had been mangled in a logging accident and could not be saved. Infection had already set in, so it was amputation or a painful and lingering death for the man. He was one of Musbewi's Galaon tribe, a people that lived upriver. Hope's steamboat would be arriving there later in the day.

Schweitzer knew that Musbewi did a lot of business with Adam Hope. The headman was a wily old man, well capable of holding his own with any colonial trader. Musbewi had shown some hostility to Lambaréné in the past. He preferred the old ways of his witch doctors. A white man appearing out of the blue, one that offered new ways and new solutions, was an obvious threat to his authority.

Gillespie was in Musbewi's village now, visiting with Mr. Collins, the American missionary working in that area. Collins had brought his wife with him. Schweitzer thought this rather unwise, but Collins, if somewhat naïve, had commitment and drive, and they were two of the essential qualities to survive in the interior. Another was faith.

Joseph had enough French to get by, and could act as a translator for the patients. This was a real boon, as communication problems were a constant thorn in the doctor's side.

Schweitzer followed Joseph into the hospital. He had carried out numerous amputations now, but they never got any easier.

'Has my saw been thoroughly cleaned?' Schweitzer asked.

'Of course, Doctor.'

'Good.'

But he would check and clean it again, for the need for hygiene had been particularly hard to instil in the local population.

The patient was a man of about forty, although age was difficult to gauge in the people here. They grew old far too quickly, at prey to the many threats the primeval forest could throw at them. Everything from malaria and dengue fever to diseases that Schweitzer could not yet name. Then came all the mishaps that might afflict jungle dwellers. Many creatures bit and stung people here, and the logging industry added to their woes. Huge logs floating in fast-moving water were the source of many accidents. Schweitzer was dealing with the results of one today.

The patient's right arm and hand had been shattered, and the bones crushed. He had made his own way to the hospital, a journey of many hours. Schweitzer could not even imagine the pain the man must have been in, but ether had been administered and his suffering eased. He would lose his arm but would live, and at least he had come to the hospital, and not trusted to his local medicine man, or *oganga*, as they were called here. They were a thorn in Schweitzer's side and in his mind they were as dangerous as they were useless. For him, they had the time-honoured qualities of total incompetence allied to cunning and controlling natures. Schweitzer thought that they would do very well as politicians in Europe.

The injured man watched Schweitzer with a mixture of trust and fear, his wide eyes darting around the room. He saw strange instruments, and probably imagined them to be instruments of torture,

Schweitzer went through his pre-amputation checklist whilst Joseph increased the ether dosage until those large eyes closed, and the patient was ready.

Heat was gathering outside as the sun rose higher in the sky. It was always punishing, and he felt its power now as sweat collected under his shirt. He had made the surgery as light and airy as he could, but the sun ruled in this land.

'Hand me the saw, Joseph, we are ready to begin.'

This was a time when stoic commitment was most needed. Today Schweitzer hummed a Bach fugue to himself, making sure he got every measure right. He found his muse aided his concentration rather than hindered it. Joseph wiped the doctor's brow with a cloth as he worked, but it could not stop droplets of sweat falling onto the patient. Thirty minutes later, the operation was over and the arm removed.

'Another job *très bien,* sir,' Joseph murmured. He had a smattering of English now, because he heard a lot of it when Schweitzer talked to Gillespie. It was starting to merge with his French, so that he often talked in his own kind of patois. Schweitzer had never spoken to Joseph in German, for that would have only confused the man further.

Schweitzer washed his hands and stayed with the amputee until he came round from the ether. The patient was puzzled at first, and then startled to see one arm gone. He gazed at where his arm should be with a mixture of longing and dread.

'Joseph, tell him that his life is saved, and tell him all that I have taught you about keeping wounds clean. He'll be able to stay here for a few days, as I'll need to change the dressing before he goes home.'

Joseph nodded, but he knew that what this man feared most was the inability to do his work and feed his family. There was not much sympathy afforded cripples here.

As Joseph shouted out what seemed more like orders than guidance to the patient, Schweitzer went to his study to get his pipe and tobacco. He sat outside the house in the shade of the veranda, if simple wooden planking could be called that.

The house cat joined him. It did not yet have a name, as he had not gotten around to giving it one. It was a cat of middle age, mainly black but with a smudge of white on its chest that looked like a bow tie. It had joined him when the *Alemba* had last arrived. The cat had jumped ship and chosen to live with him at Lambaréné. It had the run of the place now, much to the disgust of Joseph and the other helpers, some of whom would rather see the cat in a pot than as a pet.

Schweitzer fondled the head of the cat as he sucked on his pipe. The smoke went well with the cracked purr of his companion. He could feel the adrenalin needed to saw off a man's arm leaving him as he closed his eyes against the sun.

Another invaluable shipment Adam Hope had brought up on his steamboat was a large chest filled with empty tins and bottles of all shapes and sizes. Because of the permanent dampness here, it was next to impossible to store medicines in cardboard boxes, so Schweitzer had appealed to friends in Paris for help, and now they had delivered it. He had enough containers to last him out the year, if he was careful.

Schweitzer smiled as he thought of one friend in particular scurrying around to everyone he could think of, demanding tins and bottles. He relied on so many favours for Lambaréné, donations of every kind, from money to medicines, and now empty bottles. He added his book royalties to donations, and this was just enough to enable Lambaréné to move forward, despite the constant struggle.

Schweitzer finished his smoke and went back inside. Hopefully there would not be another amputation for some time. The rest of the day would involve treating the many scabies cases that came to the hospital. It was the scourge of the tribes here, driving many people crazy with the extreme itching the disease caused.

In his first time at Lambaréné he once had a man walk twenty miles to the hospital, scratching every part of his body raw as he did so. Fortunately scabies was one of the easier diseases to treat, if he could trust his patients to do what he said, which was smothering the affected areas with the ointment he had prepared. It stopped the itching within two days and made him a god in the eyes of some, a magician in the eyes of others.

The people here always referred to any illness as a 'worm' inside them. The worm sufficed for anything from mild skin diseases to more serious things, like sleeping sickness, the deadly gift of the tsetse fly. Schweitzer knew ogangas had instilled this ignorance in their people for generations; it helped bend them to their will. They were skilled psychologists who knew how to link superstition to fear, and keep it active.

The first time Schweitzer had arrived at Lambaréné, a year before the war, everything had been a steep learning curve. He had been determined not to make the mistakes of so many missionaries before him. Schweitzer knew he had his faults, just like any other man. It was hard to change the ideas that had been instilled in him since childhood, but awareness of the need to do so was the first step.

His work at Lambaréné was what God wanted him to do, of that he was sure, but it had to be tempered with pragmatism. His faith was his rock, it supported him and made him grow and drove him on. Helene shared that with him, which made them a perfect match.

Gillespie would be back in a few days. He enjoyed the man's company and conversation as much as he needed his help with the patients. Five ravaged faces turned hopefully towards Schweitzer as he re-entered the surgery. It would be another long afternoon.

*

The *River Ghost* made slow but steady progress upriver, about the same speed as a hippo on a mission. The Ogowe never ceased to amaze me in its complexity. It was a maze of tributaries, rivulets and all sorts of run-offs that few Europeans had seen, many of which were too dangerous for my steamboat to navigate. She could handle much shallower waters than old paddleboats like the *Alemba*, but I still had to be careful.

Sometimes, when we passed an unknown stretch of water leading further into the interior, I longed to steam up it, just to see what might be around the next bend. Julius always cautioned against it, wagging a finger in my face like a frustrated schoolmaster. It wasn't just the vagaries of the river that concerned him, but also the human dangers that might be lurking along its banks.

'Man get lost there, boss,' he said to me once.

I soon found out that *lost* had another, more deadly meaning for the tribes here. *Lost* meant to be killed, and maybe even eaten by a rival tribe. Despite the colonial authorities' best efforts, it still went on here. Africa might not really be the Dark Continent, but it was certainly a complex one.

Perhaps I had not made the best choice to come out here, with regards to my own problems, but I was here now. The decision had been taken, and my inheritance spent, so I was determined to make the best of it. I felt that somehow Africa held my destiny, and meeting Schweitzer had only reinforced this, but in a way I could not yet understand.

Pieters finally surfaced, jerking me out of my thoughts with his usual bellow. He joined me on deck, a little shaky, and showing all the signs of a first-class hangover.

'God, my head's got a hammer working away in it,' Pieters said.

'Good,' I murmured.

'What's that?'

'I said it's good you're finally back in the land of the living.'

'It doesn't feel like it.'

Pieters ran a hand through his face bristles, further reddening the skin beneath. A purple shadow was taking root around his nose, spreading out like a stain.

'God, even on the edge of the rainy season this sun is a killer,' Pieters said. 'How long before you stop this tub?'

'Not long, thirty minutes maybe. I suggest you get some coffee from the galley, and some food inside you. A wash wouldn't go amiss either.'

Pieters' bleary eyes tried to focus on me, but with the glare of the sun and his hung-over state it was just too much effort for him. He waved a listless hand and went below again, which suited me. Pieters was a nuisance on the bridge.

We were nearing my destination, the camp of a tribe controlled by Musbewi, a headman of the Galoan people. Their numbers had been greatly diminished in the last hundred years, through a mixture of poverty, disease, and fighting between the tribes. Musbewi had survived by cunning and violent control. He was an unpredictable man, but I rather enjoyed doing business with him. It was a good test of wills.

The key was to always let Musbewi think he was coming out ahead. Rotgut rum and a few francs were a poor exchange for quality hardwood timber. To ease my conscience I always brought a chest of small gifts to give to his people. This infuriated the other traders. They saw any act of kindness to the locals as an act of weakness. Mr. *Good* Hope, some of them called me, and they did not mean it as a compliment.

We were approaching our goal, and there was just enough banking here for the *River Ghost* to moor up. Julius barked orders to all and sundry as Pieters re-appeared. It looked like he had dashed some water into his face and drunk a few mugs of coffee.

The barge I had left here a few months ago was still in its place alongside the riverbank. It looked safe enough. This is what I used to transport teak logs to the coast. Teak was cut into smaller, more manageable sizes than the lesser quality woods. The barge could accommodate these, and the *River Ghost* had just enough power to tow them down river.

Musbewi was not amongst the crowd gathered at the riverside to greet us. He'd expect me to go to him, to stand before him as he sat on that ridiculously ornate chair the French had given him. The authorities were quite good at local politics. They knew how to play one tribe against the other, as the riches of Gabon were steadily plundered.

Because the *River Ghost* had been laid up, and expensive to repair, there was not much free stuff to give away this time. Julius distributed what we had. He strode around like a lord of the manor, loving the attention of the women as he gave out cutlery, blankets and the colourful scarves they all loved. I had soon realised that appearance and one-upmanship were king in society here. Another characteristic was the very thin skin of the men. The slightest thing could be taken as an insult.

I noticed that Pieters had taken a few things from Julius and was looking for a suitable young girl to be a beneficiary of his largesse. I would have to watch him here.

A white man approached me. A tall thin man in a crisp white shirt and matching trousers, like an elongated Schweitzer. This was Tom Collins.

'Hi there,' the man said, thrusting out a hand, 'nice to see you again, Mr. Hope.'

As I took his firm hand I wondered if this man knew his name had been given to a famous cocktail. But looking Collins up and down I was pretty sure he had no idea such a thing even existed. I returned his smile as Pieters joined us.

'Ah,' Collins said, grasping Pieters' slightly unwilling hand, 'is this your colleague?'

'Not exactly,' I said.

'Have you come up from Lambaréné?' Collins asked.

'We have.'

'Well, you've just missed Mr. Gillespie, Dr. Schweitzer's new assistant. He's gone to another camp upriver, by dugout. Charming man, that. We had a great talk about Schweitzer's book on Jesus. Neither of us really agrees with the doctor's hypotheses, but Schweitzer is truly a great theologian.'

'I'm sure he is.'

My eyes were already looking around for timber. Some logs had been secured on the river next to the barge, but not as many as I had expected. Musbewi surely had more logs ready than this.

Trading for timber was a curious affair in Gabon, and I'd had to learn the ropes quickly. Traders paid half the agreed price up front, and the locals delivered the larger logs in makeshift rafts to Cape Lopez. They would collect their second payment on the coast.

To say this was a risky and haphazard system was an understatement. Logs often failed to arrive, sometimes because of disasters on the journey, but more often skulduggery on the part of the headmen here. Sometimes, clever operators like Musbewi sold a shipment several times over to different traders, and there were many ways poor quality timber could be disguised to the inexperienced eye. The logs already floating in the river were not what I was looking for, which was teak. Teak always fetched the best price to the French money-men at the docks, and Musbewi's area was full of it.

'Mr. Pieters, you must meet my wife Ann,' Collins said. 'We are together here — all the way from Kansas.'

Collins was one of the missionaries that were present in outposts along the river, but Americans were rare here. Tom and Ann Collins had a smattering of French, although their grasp of the language was not much better than Musbewi's.

On cue, Mrs. Collins approached us, but she was not alone. Another woman was with her, a striking figure in a dark blue dress that went well against the lighter blue of the sky. I'd never seen her before.

'This is my wife Ann,' Collins said, 'and can I introduce Amie Moreau, all the way from Paris. She is a writer and she's staying with us for a while.'

What was a writer doing out here? I was immediately intrigued.

The two women were quite a contrast. Ann Collins was short and rather plump, whereas Mlle Moreau was tall and willowy, her pale complexion enhanced by her long black hair. Pieters' attention was immediately caught.

'I am more a journalist, actually,' she said, in English, which rather spoilt my intention to show off my French.

'What brings you here?' I asked. 'You must have come up on the *Alemba*?'

'I did.'

'To a God-forsaken place like this?' Pieters said. 'Why would you want to do that, a good-looking women like you?'

How I would have liked to punch Pieters in his sagging gut, but Amie Moreau ignored him.

'Perhaps we can talk later, Monsieur,' she said to me. 'I'd love to hear about your experiences here.'

'Oh, he's had a lot of *them*,' Pieters said.

'Would you gentlemen like some refreshment?' Collins said. 'My wife's home-made lemonade is a legend.'

'Mr. Pieters would love some,' I said, 'he adores lemonade, but first I have to talk with Musbewi. Perhaps I could join you all later?'

'Sure thing.'

I hoped the American could pay me what he owed as I shepherded Pieters away with them. I didn't want him anywhere near my business dealings. He would get Musbewi's back up in no time at all.

As I walked up a small incline towards the headman's dwelling I realised that the Frenchwoman had not answered my question. I was followed by an assorted bunch of villagers, all talking loudly at once.

Musbewi was sitting on his throne-like chair outside his bamboo hut, the largest in the village, but that wasn't saying much. Behind him, his *oganga* peered out of the gloom of the hut. I could see his eyes gleaming. If looks could kill I would be dead before I opened my mouth. He saw every white man as a threat, and who could say that he was wrong?

Musbewi looked like a wizened old man, but he was probably not yet fifty. The sun and environment aged people very quickly here, but his eyes were still full of fire and mischief. He grinned when I got close, showing off the few teeth he had left.

'Ah, the Hope man come to trade,' Musbewi said. 'Welcome, welcome.'

Musbewi moved his chair back a little, so that he was just out of the noonday sun, whilst I was trapped in it.

'Where wood?' I said. 'There is not enough ready for me.'

I gestured towards the river banking, waving an arm extravagantly, which I know Musbewi liked. With him everything was a pantomime, and I had a leading role in it. As I turned towards the river I noticed in the corner of my eye the Frenchwoman looking on from afar. Her hand-on-hip stance was quizzical. I would have to be careful with her. A journalist could mean anything. She might even be a French official secretly nosing around.

Musbewi put on his official hat, the one he always wore when dealing with white men. It had been a top hat once but was so battered it looked like a shapeless black mass merging with his head.

'You want more?' Musbewi said, 'more of wood?'

His French was colourful, but I could always get his drift. It was a long fifteen minutes of horse-trading in the sun before a deal was struck. Musbewi used every gesture of his act, and a few new ones I hadn't even seen before. He smiled, scowled, displayed mock or real anger, and called me a French devil out to cheat a poor soul like him, until I gradually upped my price, to the level that I had always expected to pay.

I looked crestfallen at his victory and Musbewi was delighted he had won again. He clapped his hands and shouted until a few of his women appeared with refreshments. They offered me a large platter of unwashed fruit and what looked like monkey meat. I had no intention of touching any of it.

As I had suspected, the old chief had many logs of teak stacked up in a clearing behind his hut, all of which I had agreed to buy. They had already been cut into the right size.

'You have raft ready for the other wood?' I said.

'Yes, raft ready.'

'Okay. Tell your men to start tomorrow, then, before the big rains come.'

They would tie the large logs floating at the riverbank together into a makeshift platform, and then raft it all the way down to Cape Lopez. Well, that was the usual plan, but it was a plan that sometimes went awry. The river could prove too much for some rafts, and hippos also saw them as a challenge. I once saw a raft overturned when a hippo came up underneath it, leaving the men who fell into the river at its mercy.

Twelve cases of rum and a modest amount of French francs sealed the deal. Now I needed to get the money Collins owed me to pay for the logs. I would get at least five times what I paid Musbewi for the timber at Cape Lopez, and the Hope Trading Company would be back up and running again.

Julius had been watching my dealings from a distance, and as soon as I gestured to him, he started to organise the loading of timber onto the barge. Musbewi's men would help, and very soon the camp would be alive with singing as they laboured.

I went to find Pieters, I didn't want him straying around this camp too much, for that man attracted trouble like a magnet did iron filings. I wanted to talk money with Collins alone. With the offer of another bottle of rum I managed to get Pieters to go back to the *Ghost* to toast my business success.

'Make sure it's only one bottle,' I said.

'I have your money, Mr. Hope,' Collins said, 'if you'd care to come up to the house. Interesting man, that Pieters.'

'Yes, you could say that.'

Collins' use of the word *house* was somewhat optimistic. His place was more a shed on stilts. It was like a smaller version of Schweitzer's at Lambaréné, with a corrugated metal roof that would encourage the sun to do its worst. Ann Collins was waiting for us in the doorway, her squat figure silhouetted against the dark interior. As I was ushered inside I braced myself for her famed soft drink and wondered where the Frenchwoman was.

*

Schweitzer sat at his piano. It was an upright that had been specially made for him in Paris, in a way that it might better withstand the African climate. He moved his hands over the keyboard and closed his eyes. Music was his salve, and the piano a strong link to his former life. Schweitzer viewed his past as a sturdy companion, because it was a good one. When his time here without his wife became very hard, the piano was always there for him. It was a constant presence in his life, and losing himself in a Bach piece took away all the cares of his day, at least for a little while.

It was a better evening than most at Lambaréné. Usually there was very little breeze to be had here, but tonight, as the wet season was imminent, there was enough to move the turgid air around, and even freshen it up a little.

Schweitzer thought back to the time before the war when he'd had to go to Cape Lopez for medical treatment himself. He'd had an abscess that would not heal at Lambaréné. Helene went with him and how they had enjoyed the sea breezes of the coast. It had seemed like a holiday to them, despite his troublesome tooth.

Schweitzer played a fugue in B Minor, and the melancholy nature of that key suited his mood that night. He played a transcription of the piece by Liszt, of which he approved. Usually he used his own, written in Paris in that decade when his passion for Bach had all but consumed him.

The piano projected out into the African night, a brittle but sweet sound. Schweitzer wondered what the night creatures thought of it. As he played, he could hear the solid thrum of forest life all, but it did not disturb his concentration. Rather it enhanced it, and blended in as he brought the music to life.

Schweitzer played on for an hour, than felt the need for a pipe before sleep. It was not wise to sit outside in the night here, such was the profusion of mosquitoes, but with the help of his pungent tobacco smoke to keep them away, he thought he'd risk it.

He sat on the same wooden step he usually shared with the cat, but it wasn't around this night. It would be on the prowl somewhere, a very dangerous activity for a creature so small and unsuited for the environment here. Cats were usually leopard-sized here, but his wily feline friend had survived so far. A name for the cat came to him. He would call him Sebastian, and hoped his muse would not be offended.

For a while Schweitzer smoked calmly, blowing small clouds of smoke around his head whenever he heard the whine of a mosquito close by. He liked to listen to the cacophony of evening sounds, particularly the calling of night birds. There was a myriad of them that seemed to master all keys and octaves as they cried out over the constant whirr of insects. All around him lay the black wall of the jungle. He could hear it sway and heave in the breeze, not so much a shifting mass but more a solid creature of nature.

Some sounds were not so welcome. A scream pierced the night, supported by a burst of nervous chatter from the birds. Schweitzer knew a small creature had just perished in this savage world. A sharp shriek as life was snatched away in an instant, taken by something bigger and stronger. Nature's way.

Was the scream just an instinctive reaction, or did animals also fear death, even if they could never foresee it? It was a question that Schweitzer had often pondered from early childhood. Once he'd argued with a young friend because that boy had insisted on killing songbirds. That was back home in Alsace, amidst countryside so very different to the landscape of Gabon. His homeland was safe, clean and ordered, that most of all, and it had nurtured his early life, not threatened it.

Gradually, Schweitzer's thoughts turned to Adam Hope, the Englishman with the Old Testament name. He was interested in this man, because Hope was different, and men who were different were quite rare. He had learned this some years ago, for he knew he was different himself. From scholarly musician and theologian, to doctor, and then missionary, was quite a journey, and most of his friends had cautioned against it. You are a Bach expert, they said, a fine organist who has built up a large following. You are a successful author, so why give all that up, why change your life in such a drastic way?

Schweitzer knew his decision to come to Lambaréné had amazed and worried his friends, all except Helene of course. She knew it was his faith that underpinned his new life.

He had felt the need to help others since he was a boy, but for a long time he'd put this down to the vanity of a young, unformed mind. He'd concentrated on his musical and intellectual progression, but rather than diminish with age, this desire grew, like a plant thrusting its way out of the earth, until he knew that it was God speaking to him, telling him to act. So he had done so, choosing medicine as his means to an end, which was Africa, and Lambaréné in particular. This was his destiny, and he embraced it.

Adam Hope had suffered in the war. It was written in his face, in his eyes that never settled on anything for long; but other, older pain was also there. Schweitzer imagined a disappointing life, maybe a rudderless and lonely life. To receive love as a child was everything, and perhaps this man had never had it. Schweitzer's own childhood had been rich and fulfilling. It had prepared him to be the man he now was.

Religion had not been discussed in their first meeting but he sensed that Hope might be an atheist, or at last purported to be. It would explain his unease around the mission. Atheism was something Schweitzer had tried to understand, but he had never quite managed it. How could a man fill that void, what could compensate for being without God? As usual, too many thoughts crowded into his head. They always did at the end of each day, but one by one they were pushed out by the need to sleep.

*

Mrs. Collins' lemonade was better than expected, and she'd somehow found a way of keeping it cool. She served it with small scones she'd also made, plus strawberry jam she'd brought all the way from Kansas. Cream would have completed the country club scene, but cream was impossible here.

I dealt with financial matters quickly, just in case Pieters showed up again.

'I'm sorry it's taken so long,' Collins said, handing me a crisp bundle of francs. 'If you'd care to count it, Mr. Hope, I can then put the money in an envelope for you.'

I handed the money back to him. 'I don't need to count it, but an envelope would be good.'

As Collins rummaged around his untidy table I detached a few of the notes, and put them down alongside my lemonade glass.

'A small donation for your mission here.'

'Why, Mr. Hope,' Ann said, her face beaming, 'that is *so* kind of you.'

The Frenchwoman joined us. As I stood up, I instinctively pushed back my too-long hair. and wished I had shaved today.

'Hello again.' I said.

She acknowledged me with a slight smile.

'Ah, there you are, Amie,' Ann said. 'I'll make some fresh coffee for us all.'

'Did your business go well, Mr. Hope?' Amie said.

'Yes, well enough,' I answered. 'It's good to get back to the logging. My boat has been out of action for a while.'

Now that I could see her clearly, out of the glare of the sun, Amie Moreau was a striking woman. Some might describe her as handsome rather than pretty. She had deep-set brown eyes, a strong jaw, and perfectly formed white teeth. This was such a rarity with Europeans here, as dentists were very few and far between. I flicked a tongue over my own teeth, which were still sound, but I hoped they were not too yellow. Pieters was approaching the house, so I quickly pocketed the money.

'Ah, here's the charming Mr. Pieters,' Amie said. 'Is he your partner in the timber trade?'

'Hardly. Pieters has a boat repair business of sorts down on the coast. He does work for me from time to time.'

'Then why is he here?'

'Mr. Pieters likes to travel up river now and then.'

Pieters announced his presence just as I felt the conversation was about to become awkward. Amie Moreau intrigued me, but I was not used to being asked questions out here, and she asked a lot of them.

The Collinses had put on as much of a spread as possible. It might not have meant much to a Parisienne like Moreau but it did to me, and even more to Pieters.

'Good God,' Pieters said, 'roast chicken. I haven't had that for a while.'

'We keep chickens here,' Ann Collins said. 'For the eggs, you know.'

'Dr. Schweitzer has them at Lambaréné too,' Collins added. 'In fact, when he first came out here, the first building he turned into a hospital was an old chicken shed. Isn't that remarkable?'

I was thankful to have a good evening meal for once, but I was bored already with the banal chat. The table was too small for five people and we were hunched over it like crows over a carcass.

As we ate Pieters held court. He treated us to a potted history of his life, ten percent of which was probably true. I knew he was thirsting for a proper drink, not poor quality rum, but there was no chance of that here, any more than there had been at Lambaréné. With sweat beading his forehead Pieters was about to embark on his thin range of risqué jokes until a well-aimed kick from me stopped him. The Collinses were oblivious to this, but Amie noticed it. She hid a smile behind her hand.

'You are very quiet, Mr. Hope,' she said.

'Am I? Well, it's been rather a long day.'

'I'm sure it has. So, how long have you been out here?'

'Four years now.'

'You must have been in the war though?'

'Amie, don't quiz the man,' Ann said, as she ordered plates to be cleared away to make room for what she proudly called the dessert.

'Amie here is a regular news hound,' Collins said.

'What are *you* doing here?' I asked Amie.

'I work freelance for various magazines back home. French people increasingly want to know what's going on in

73

our colonies. It's not just you British who have a sense of empire, you know.'

'Tell him about your book too,' Ann said.

'Book?'

'Yes, Amie is writing a novel.'

'Well, I'm not actually writing it yet,' Amie said.

'I tried to read a novel once,' Pieters said. 'It was boring, so I gave up after a few pages. I'm a man that likes to get things done, rather than read about other people doing stuff.'

Yes, like lying dead drunk in a stinking bed all day, I thought. Pieters was starting to get agitated. Most drunks did. The dessert arrived, a selection of local fruits, and more lemonade to go with it. This was the push Pieters needed to leave the table, making it rattle as he did so.

'I got to get back to the boat,' he said. 'Uh, I just remembered, I need to check something in the engine.'

He was gone before Mrs. Collins could entreat him to stay, but it was obvious none of us were sorry to see him depart.

'He seems like a man on a mission,' Collins said.

'Yes, you could call it that,' I said, as a sliced up an *atanga*, a fruit from a kind of pear tree that grew here. Ann Collins left us to supervise the coffee making, and soon Collins joined her. I guessed they were a couple that never left each other's side for long.

'So what will your novel be about?' I said, looking into Amie's eyes for the first time.

'Oh, writers never want to talk about what they are working on. We are a superstitious lot.'

'Are you? I met a few officers in the army who wrote poetry. They couldn't *stop* talking.'

'Well, maybe poets feel the need. They are such sensitive souls.'

'If you say so. Have you started your book? I guess it must be set here, because here you are.'

'It will be set in a few places.'

'This will be your first book?'

'My first novel, yes. I've been writing for magazines since the end of the war.'

'Ah, the end of the war. One of my men copped it just days before it finished.'

'Copped it?'

'He was killed. It somehow sums up the senseless of it all, doesn't it?'

'Indeed.'

The fierce sun of Gabon had already worked some creases around Amie's dark eyes, but she still looked too pale, even for a European city dweller. She had a habit of pulling at her lower lip in between sentences. I wasn't sure if this was meant to be coquettish or not, but it did attract me. All sorts of things ran through my mind.

'Lost in your thoughts?' Amie asked.

'Sorry. It's a bad habit of mine. I'm not used to intelligent company, or a meal as good as the one we've just had.'

'You were an officer then? In the war, I mean.'

'Was I?'

'Yes, you just referred to your fellow soldiers as *my men.*'

Watkins was the man who died two days before the guns fell silent for good. I could still see him vividly, just the moment before he lost the top of his head. He was the last of the company's casualties. Watkins had just brought me a mug of tea and was making his way back down the trench. There was a good mood amongst the men that morning. There'd been no gunfire for days, and we all knew the end was very close. This led to carelessness with some, despite my best efforts to prevent it. Watkins hadn't kept low enough and he attracted the attention of a German sniper. They were pretty good, too. Quite deadly, in fact.

When Watkins fell back, with a shocked look on his face as his head disintegrated, it was as if he was symbolizing all the carnage of that war, and the utter bloody futility of it. By the time his parents got the telegram everyone dreaded, the war was over. They would have been out in the street celebrating with friends and neighbours, rejoicing that their boy had come through it.

'I'm sorry,' Amie said, 'I see that you don't want to talk about the war.'

Tom Collins joined us again, which was a relief. He brought a large coffee pot with him, followed by his wife with a tray of fresh china cups.

'We like to serve coffee to our guests personally. The boys here never seem to get it right.'

Like Pieters, I wished that I had something to stiffen the coffee, for Billy Watkins would stay with me for the rest of the day.

'So how long are you staying here?' I asked Amie.

'I'm not sure yet.'

'You're welcome to stay with us as long as you want,' Ann said. 'I'd be glad of the company. And your donation was very kind.'

'Yes, funds are always a problem,' Collins added. 'When I visit Dr. Schweitzer at Lambaréné we spend a lot of time bemoaning our mutual poverty.'

'But God always provides in the end,' Ann said.

I caught Amie's eyes. They said that she didn't believe this one iota. The Collinses were zealot-like, and fervour in people, any kind of fervour, had always unnerved me somewhat. I'd seen enough of it before, as wave after wave of young officers arrived at the front full of it, only to have it quickly knocked out of them — if they survived more than a few weeks, that is. Being keen meant you could be used, and no one would do that to me again.

I drank the rather good coffee, and thought what strange company I was keeping lately. First Schweitzer and now the Collins duo. I was not yet sure what kind of company Amie Moreau might be. I was not sure she'd be any company at all.

*

Schweitzer was reading a new letter from his wife. It was the fourth time he had read it in the last week, and its pages were starting to show signs of wear. He devoured each word, particularly the news about Rhena.

Schweitzer put the photograph Helene had sent of Rhena on the piano. It was taken on her fifth birthday, and showed a happy little girl staring into the camera. The photograph would keep better if he put it in a box, but he wanted to see it every day. In the moist air of the jungle it would soon start to yellow, but he'd ask Helene to send more. If he wasn't able to see his daughter growing up, at least he could see images of her progress.

Leaving his family behind had been his biggest sacrifice so far, but he doubted Rhena could ever come out until she was much older. There was too much danger here, and he wanted her to have as good an education as he'd been afforded. Knowledge was everything. He had known that by the time he was ten, and it had paved the way for his mission in life.

Schweitzer was disturbed by a commotion outside. Night was starting to fall, and excited voices were calling out. Joseph came running up.

'Big cat in camp, Doctor. Come quick. Bring gun.'

Schweitzer did have two hunting rifles at the mission, supplied by a French supporter on the coast, and he knew how to use them. A leopard, prowling around the chicken coop, was causing the fuss. It happened quite often.

'Has it got at the chickens?' he asked.

'No, all the boys shout and it go away.'

'Well, there's no need to be so excited then, is there?'

'It will come back, sir. So you shoot it then, yes?'

Schweitzer was prepared to shoot an animal, if it was really necessary, but he hoped that he'd never have to shoot a leopard. He'd come face to face with one once, in his first time at Lambaréné. He'd been exploring the local area and the cat had calmly appeared out of the bush. They had eyed each other up with what Schweitzer liked to think was mutual respect, but it was more likely fear. He'd been unarmed that day, although he'd been urged to take a rifle with him if he was walking into the jungle.

That had been quite an introduction to Lambaréné and the wilderness that surrounded it. He'd looked into the piercing green eyes of the leopard and knew that God would keep him safe. Schweitzer did not move a muscle, and the stand-off lasted at least a minute before the cat turned away with a dismissive snarl. It disappeared into the undergrowth, the mottled patterns on its coat immediately making it as one with its surroundings.

A few of his patients that should be resting in their hut were up and about, looking fearful and talking loudly. They wanted to see Schweitzer carrying a rifle, but he shouted to them that the leopard had gone and they were all safe. The hens soon settled down again, and the night returned to its blend of more usual sounds.

Schweitzer went back into the house, where he was torn by the need to write back to Helene, play the piano, and sleep.

*

The deal with Musbewi done and the meal with the Collinses over, I went back to the *River Ghost*. Pieters was not on board, but I was too tired to think much about it. Navigating the river was arduous. I had to look out for so many things. Dangerous currents, eddies, sometimes even whirlpools that could pull the boat around and disorientate the helmsman. Then came the submarine-sized hippos. I'm sure male hippos thought the *River Ghost* was a strange challenger newly arrived on the water, because they always took exception to my passing. Fortunately, the size of the boat, and the noise of its engine, usually deterred them from a direct attack.

I thought I was having a nightmare when Julius woke me. He was shaking me by the shoulder and shouting in my ear. My initial reaction was to reach up and grasp him around the neck, which made him even more agitated.

'For God's sake man, what is it?'

'Boss, come quick! Pieters man in big trouble. He lost if boss don't come quick.'

Hearing Julius' use of the word *lost* I became alert very quickly.

Julius had already taken my Colt revolver from its drawer. I never kept it loaded, so I had to fumble around for my box of bullets whilst trying to put a shirt on.

All the while Julius was shouting, and changing from French to Galoan every other word. I did hear *woman* a lot though, which could only mean one thing where Pieters was concerned.

I rushed back to the camp with Julius. It was awash with shouting and people running around. A crowd of angry men and baying women had gathered outside a hut that had a flimsy wooden door.

'He there, boss,' Julius shouted. 'He hide because they want kill him.'

Pieters must have been cowering behind the door because I could feel a weight stopping it opening, and hear his strained breathing.

Menacing faces glared at me and some men jeered. A few carried torches, and the guttering flames made their eyes gleam in the dark night. Everyone saw the gun in my hand.

In a situation like this I knew only the gun's fear factor was any good. If this situation worsened, I'd only have a few seconds to use it before the crowd was on me. All my old training clicked into place. Don't show fear. Stick to your task. I could hear the bellowing voice of my first sergeant major at officer training.

A man with a spear was trying to break into the hut, but I pushed him away with the Colt almost in his face. He thought about attacking me but was pulled away by others. I wondered where Musbewi was, or Collins for that matter, but it was better that the missionary wasn't here. His presence would only complicate matters.

I stood as close to the hut's door as I could and shouted.

'You in there, Pieters?'

'That you, Hope? Yes, of course I'm fucking in here. They almost killed me.'

'What the hell have you been up to this time?'

'It's just a misunderstanding. I didn't know her husband was around. I didn't even know she had a husband. I was just asking her if she liked her scarf and this man burst in. Jabbed at me with a spear. Got me in the arm. I'm bleeding like a pig in here.'

As he said this I saw the bloodstains all over the door, gleaming black in the moonlight. So, this was really a case of seduction, maybe even rape, to be paid for with a scarf. It had happened before with Pieters, a few years ago, down on the coast. He'd only been showing someone's young daughter a trinket then too.

'Tell the crowd to get back,' I told Julius. Women pulled their children away, and most faded back into the night. They did not want trouble with whites, but their men were more resolute. They stood quietly now, bunched together with arms folded, waiting for this drama to develop.

I had to get Pieters back to the boat, but I felt more like shooting him than saving him. The spearman should have done a better job.

'Julius, is this the man who attacked him?' I nodded at the spearman.

'Yes, him there, boss, but they all want Pieters man lost now.'

I turned to face Pieters' attacker. He was bare-chested and obviously up for the fight. His eyes were glaring, catching the light of the torches, but he too was fixated on the gun.

Musbewi appeared. Trust that man to have perfect timing. He had his official crumpled top hat on, and behind him trailed his *oganga*. The enraged husband moved to stand next to his chief. I doubted that Musbewi cared much about what might have happened to a young girl here. He was weighing up how this could benefit him.

I hoped Collins was armed, just in case this escalated. Most missionaries were, this far inland. Musbewi gestured towards me and then turned his back to face the crowd. In his high-pitched, rather tremulous voice, he harangued them with a speech about God knows what. It was probably something about the evils of white men, which was very fertile territory indeed. As Musbewi made his pitch, I quietly told Pieters to come out.

'Is is safe?' he whispered.

'Just come out, man. I'm armed. We have to get to the boat as quickly as possible, before they lose their fear of the gun. Can you walk okay?'

'Yeah, it's just my arm, but I've lost a lot of blood.'

'Julius, help Pieters when he comes out.'

Pieters opened the door and stepped out shakily. His left arm hung down by his side, blood dripping from it, but it looked like nothing vital had been cut. If it had been he would have bled out long ago.

A loud murmur went up from the crowd, and Musbewi spun around with a pointing arm. The *oganga* was chanting something in the background, and he had the attention of the man with the spear. With Julius pushing Pieters on in front we started to make our way back to the river. It would be a long few hundred yards.

It went well for a while. The crowd parted and we made about fifty yards before the spearman made his move. With a yell he raced towards us. He was lit up by the flickering torchlight of the villagers, spear thrust out ahead of him like a bayonet on a Lee Enfield.

I raised my free hand and shouted for him to stop. He was planning to run Pieters through and he ignored me. Pieters stood as if frozen in time. All the bravado had ebbed out of the man along with his blood, and he was truly a man transfixed. I shouted out a few more times, panic rising in me like bile.

The 44 Colt was a beast of a gun, capable of stopping an elephant if used correctly. It jumped in my hand as I shot once, hitting the man in his chest and hurling him backwards. He was dead before he hit the ground, with a fist-sized hole in his chest.

Death can happen in the blink of an eye and it just had. This was the first time I had used the Colt since the German boy, and he was with me now. His face merged with that of the spearman, bright blue eyes strangely fixed in an ebony face. I was as shocked as the crowd, and even Musbewi was struck dumb. No one else made a move towards me.

The dead man was dragged away unceremoniously by his feet. He left a strong trail of blood that was immediately latched onto by a variety of insects.

I knew this stunned lull wouldn't last, so between us we dragged and propelled Pieters towards the *River Ghost*. Julius was reluctant to do so, and I could not blame him.

I heard a groundswell of noise begin anew from the crowd, but it was now one of moaning, not anger. No one was chasing us. The Colt had worked its deadly magic.

We reached the safety of the boat, to be greeted by a collection of anxious faces peering out into the dark. The crew would go from anxiety to panic if they knew what had just happened, so I hissed at Julius to keep quiet about it.

I was close to punching Pieters but the man was just about done in. His normally red face was drained of colour and he was quiet, maybe for the first time in his life. I took a closer look at his arm in the deck light of the boat. A chunk of flesh had been chewed up but nothing vital had been severed. Julius was quite capable of attending to it.

'Take this idiot on board and patch him up. He'll live — unfortunately.'

'You come too, boss. Not safe here now.'

He was probably right but I was thinking about Amie, Collins and his wife. An incident like this would certainly give Amie something to write about. I had to go back to check on them.

I had killed a man. You could almost call it murder. A stick against a gun.

I had broken my solemn word to myself. And for what? To save a lowlife like Pieters, whose only real connection to me was the colour of his skin? I'd vowed to never take another life after that German boy. He would be the last, I'd told myself.

I felt a crushing, sickening feeling deep in the pit of my stomach, but I had to suppress it, choke it down before it overwhelmed me. This night was far from over.

Keeping the Colt pointing downwards at the ground, I walked back towards the waiting crowd. We had not been chased back to the *River Ghost*; in fact we had not even been followed. A crowd of about a hundred had stayed close to Musbewi. They were gathered behind him now in a semi-circle. As I approached them I recognised the dry copper-like taste of fear in my mouth.

If Musbewi told them to kill me it would all be over very quickly, but as I got closer I sensed the atmosphere had calmed down. There was no sign of the dead man, and the fact that I was still alive meant that Musbewi had a plan. He approached me, hesitantly at first, but with more confidence as he saw that I didn't level my gun. He raised both arms in the air, as if invoking some unknown god, and checked that all eyes were upon him.

'You pay,' he shouted. 'You pay big for lost man.'

So, it was to be money for a killing. It hardly made me feel any better.

'And man on boat,' Musbewi said. 'You give him to me.'

'Not possible,' I said. 'Tell your people to go to their beds now. There is nothing more to see tonight.'

'Then you pay more. You pay for two men.'

I could see Collins walking down from his shed-like house. His white shirt appeared out of the darkness like a signal. Musbewi saw him too. He ran to him, startling Collins so much the man almost stumbled.

'We were woken by someone hammering on our door,' Collins said. 'They say you have shot a man. Ann is very frightened.'

'It's all over now, Mr. Collins. I'll tell you my story when Musbewi calms down. It was a matter of self defence, I assure you.'

The presence of another white man, and one they obviously respected, caused what was left of the crowd to further drift away, leaving us alone with the old chief, and his ever-lurking witch doctor.

It was a strange three-way conversation-cum-shouting match for the next ten minutes. Working out a price for the dead man was like any other bargaining to Musbewi. Life was cheap along the river.

Collins was shocked, torn between solidarity with me, and his horror at the thought of me shooting a man. When he learned why Pieters had been in such danger his anxiety only increased.

'This is going to cause a lot of trouble with the French authorities here,' Collins said.

'Don't I know it.'

Musbewi did not understand English, and he became agitated again, getting closer to me, but not too close. I knew Musbewi would not want the French poking around his camp any more than I wanted them looking into me. I was here on sufferance after all, the only non-French steamboat captain here.

'This Pieters,' Collins said, 'do you think he actually, you know, with that man's wife?'

The missionary came to a halt, swallowing hard.

'We'll never get the truth from him. Once he gets over this shock he'll have a perfect story all polished up for the police.'

Collins grabbed my arm. 'That poor man. It's such a bad business, Mr. Hope.'

'Yes. It is.'

The moon had vanished, and with it the starlit sky. It was starting to rain. Just a gentle drizzle sifted through the trees, but we all knew it was the precursor to the big rains. By morning it would be heavy and relentless, but all the better for me to up anchor with the *River Ghost* and leave.

Musbewi soon got down to the question of money, and eventually I offered him the last of the rum, another dozen cases, and half of the money Collins had given me. Musbewi could barely hide his delight. I know he would have settled for less, but the thought of a long haggle disgusted me. My hypocrisy only went so far.

Musbewi conferred with his *oganga*, who was none too pleased with this arrangement. His protest took the form a little dance. His feet shuffled around in dirt that was already starting to turn muddy, but Musbewi took no notice of him.

I was exhausted. It was the same kind of tiredness I'd experienced in the trenches. The adrenalin was flowing out of my body now, to be replaced with a kind of aftershock that I hadn't experienced in years. It was as if an old enemy had me in its grip again, telling me it was back and shaking me hard. You've never really gotten away, it said. I thought about that man's wife, and no doubt children, and who would provide for them.

'Please apologise to your wife for me,' I told Collins, 'but I really had no choice. If I'd allowed Pieters to be killed, French troops would have been all over this camp like a rash. Your position would probably have been compromised, and the lives of the people here made very difficult.'

'Yes, I see that. I've always got the feeling that the French resent Protestant missions here anyway. This is all so upsetting. You said life is cheap here, Mr. Hope, but I think that means only black life.'

'Yes, I'm afraid that it does. I hope that one day that will change — but not any time soon, I think.'

'Amen to that.'

Collins ushered me away from Musbewi and spoke quietly, almost in my ear.

'My grandfather kept people from this part of the world. I'm talking about slaves, Mr. Hope. My family has tried to erase this from our history, but I was not prepared to do that. That's one of the reasons I'm here.'

I dropped my own voice and got even closer to Collins.

'Do you have a gun here?' I asked him. 'Just in case?'

'A gun? No, I don't. Maybe that's surprising for a man from Kansas, but Ann and I thought our bibles would suffice. I'm sure we are safe here, Mr. Hope.'

'You are welcome to come down the river with me.'

'No one will harm us here, despite this terrible business.'

'I'll leave in the morning, then. The *Alemba* will be coming up to Lambaréné now that the heavens are about to open. I'll report this myself to its captain.'

'There'll be an official inquiry.'

'Yes.'

I doubted that this would prove be much of a problem, once the facts were known. The French here would require plenty of form filling, and they would bluster and admonish, but in truth they would have preferred me to shoot Musbewi himself. He had become notorious in recent years in the way he cheated traders, and a bit too influential amongst his people. He was a thorn in their flesh that they would not mind being removed.

No one tried to stop me going back to the *River Ghost*. The rain was strengthening, and was now coming down in waves, was supported by an increasingly strong wind, robust enough to bend the thinnest jungle trees to its will. They began a strange, ungainly dance as if tearing at their roots, and all the undergrowth joined in.

I stood on the river banking for a long minute when I reached the boat. I wanted the elements to scour me clean, but this was a hope forlorn. A voice called out to me from the darkness.

'Boss, why you stand there like that? You all wet. Come on board.'

Julius was standing on deck. He bent down to pick up a lantern, which he used like a flashlight to faintly light up my way.

'Has anyone come near?' I said, as I clambered on board.

'No, boss. They afraid of Big Colt.'

He'd always called the gun this, since the first time I'd reluctantly shown it to him. Now that he knew its power he was probably even more enamoured with it. The first thing to do was to put Big Colt away, and this time lock the draw in which it was kept. Julius looked at me closely.

'Boss okay?'

'Yes, Boss is okay. Get some sleep now, Julius, but make sure there's a watchman on deck through the night.'

'Yes, boss.'

Julius touched me on my arm, something he had never done before.

'That Pieters man is bad man. He cause trouble for you.'

'He surely has. No matter, we leave early tomorrow, whilst we still have the timber.'

I just wanted to sleep, and hoped that oblivion would come with it. Boss was certainly not okay.

For once I was not the one having the nightmare. Pieters' screaming roused me. It roused the whole crew, and for a moment I thought the *River Ghost* was being attacked. Pieters' bunk was not far from my cabin, and within seconds I was up and holding the man by the shoulders. Julius also appeared, rubbing a sleepy hand across his face.

The Belgian had a fever.

'Got devil in him,' Julius said.

I managed to bring Pieters out of it with a few good shakes. He became quiet again, but he was still delirious, his face shining with sweat.

'There's not much else we can do for him now,' I said. 'His arm might be infected. We'd better leave him for Dr. Schweitzer, when we get down to Lambaréné. Go settle the crew down, Julius. We cast off at first light.'

The rain was really getting going now. It made staccato sounds as it hit the deck of the boat. It was a bit like the chatter of German machine guns.

Pieters sank back into a deep sleep so I left him. I went up on deck where a solid sheet of water swept down on me. It was not unpleasant. I turned my head towards the sky and let the rain soak through me. There was no sign of life in Musbewi's camp. Hopefully we could be away whilst his people stayed in their huts to keep dry.

The river would be even harder to navigate now, as it filled up with floodwater. I watched the rain merge with the Ogowe in a wild alliance of movement, and the *River Ghost* began to rock as the wind increased.

Somewhere, far off in the west, there was a single flash of lightning. It arced down onto the horizon in a giant finger of white light. Everything was lit up for a moment, until the jungle settled back into its black mystery. I felt very small, and very human, as I sensed my eyes moisten. It wasn't the rain. This hadn't happened since the last day of the war, and I had never thought it would again.

I stayed on watch until I was sure the boat was safe, then got back under cover, where I dried my head with a towel and found a cigar to smoke. I lay back on my bunk and tried to come to terms with what had happened, and what I had done.

Slowly smoking the cigar did calm me, at least for a while. I smoked it right down to the name brand encircling it. When it was finished I opened a small porthole, which immediately let the rain in. I threw the butt into the river, where it hissed for the briefest of moments and then died.

*

Julius lay on his bunk, in a cabin with the other men, apart from the one who stood guard on deck. He had the only bunk; the other men swung gently back and forth in their hammocks. The air was fetid, with many noises and smells swirling around. A stoker snored like the engines he fed, whilst another muttered constantly in his sleep. It seemed that Julius was the only one troubled by what had happened in the camp. Maybe this is what education gives a man, he thought. It made him think more, perhaps too much.

Hope had saved a man Julius knew he did not really care about. It was still a matter of colour, even for a man like Hope, who had always seemed so different to most of the whites here. He remembered the stories his grandfather used to tell him, when he was still small enough to sit on his knee. He told about the white men who came with the long sticks that killed. They were devil weapons that flashed fire and then death, but it wasn't long before his own people lusted after them, grandfather said. When he'd asked why, the old man had closed his eyes and muttered, 'Because they are power, they give you power.'

Julius wondered if he too wanted power. He certainly wanted a better life for himself one day. As he mulled over these thoughts Julius sensed someone watching him. Osobu was staring at him, his eyes gleaming, even in the gloom of their cabin. Julius stared back. Neither man spoke for a long moment.

'The boss man is just another white man,' Osobu finally muttered, as he rolled over in his hammock to show Julius his back. 'They are all the same.'

*

I was up at first light. This was a magical time for the river and the land it fed. A time of renewal and growth, or rather super-growth, for everything was outsized in the jungle. Julius brought me coffee.

'Everything okay below?' I asked him.

'All quiet, boss. Pieters man still sleeping.'

'Still feverish?'

'Not so very much now. Pity him hadn't got lost last night. He make big trouble for all of us.'

If Julius had his way, Pieters would have been quietly pushed over the side. He'd have been a skeleton within days. Nothing was wasted here and every carcass fed the system. That would have suited the authorities too, for it would mean less fuss and form filling.

Julius was swaying slightly, moving from side to side. He usually did when he was nervous. He was an impressive physical specimen, his frame silhouetted against the early morning light that streamed through my cabin door. The man glistened with health, height and strength.

'Do you want to say something else to me, Julius?'

'Boss, boys are talking.'

'What about?'

'They know you pay Musbewi big money for lost man.'

'You mean you told them I did.'

He swayed even more.

'Yes, I say. Now they worry about *their* pay.'

'Tell them there's no need to worry. Hope always pays, you know that.'

'Yes, boss.'

'Start the engine check now, and tell the cook to get some food ready.'

At least I was hungry, and found I was able to lock the killed man away like my prisoner in a cell, at least for a while. The break in the weather did not last long. As it poured down again I saw a woman approaching the boat. She was trying to shelter under a ridiculous sky-blue parasol that was meant to protect against the midday sun, not an African monsoon. It was Amie Moreau, who was the last person I wanted to see. There was no sign of Collins, though, and I was surprised he'd let her walk through the camp alone after what had happened.

The *River Ghost* would not be ready to weigh anchor for thirty minutes yet. It would take that long for the boilers to get up enough steam. As I checked the clock in the boat's cabin I could hear the stokers below singing as they fed the burners. Good Welsh steam coal was doing its job, thousands of miles away from home.

It was not yet seven o'clock, so the Frenchwoman was up very early. Suspiciously early, I thought. Suddenly, Collins did appear, struggling to catch up with Amie whilst carrying a heavy suitcase. I knew what this meant and muttered a fine series of curses, but no one heard them.

The parasol had not been much good, and Amie was soaked through. She looked cold too. The temperature had dropped from humid to almost chilly overnight. It always did when the rains came. The locals hated it.

'Mr. Hope,' she shouted over the noise of the rain, 'how do they say it in English? — permission to come aboard?'

'For what reason?'

'Can you take me downriver to Lambaréné with you? I can pay.'

Collins joined us, looking more worn than ever as he strained with the case. I wondered what the hell was in it.

'Hello, Mr. Hope. What a tragic night it was. But everything seems calm in the camp now.'

'Musbewi got what he wanted. He's a pragmatic man.'

'Indeed. I still find it very sad that life is considered so cheap here. Sometimes I'm reminded of my father's tales of the American West. It was all built on slaughter, he used to say.'

And everywhere else, I thought, but I kept my own counsel. I descended the boat's narrow walkway to take the case from Collins, and ushered Amie on board.

'Permission granted,' I muttered, 'and please don't mention money again. I've done enough bargaining on this trip to last me a lifetime. Wait here till I take this case up, then I'll come back for you. This planking can be treacherous in this weather.'

Our cook was on deck, about to call me to breakfast, so I turned him into a porter for a minute. I held out a hand to Collins, which to my relief he took, and shook firmly.

'Are you still sure you and your wife will be okay here?' I said.

'I'm certain of it. The authorities will be here within days and Musbewi will want to keep a low profile. I'm learning about local politics.'

'Okay, then. I'd appreciate it if you'd tell them I had no choice in what happened last night.'

'There's no need to ask me that, Mr. Hope. Don't worry, I will tell them the truth of the matter.'

'Thank you.'

I wanted to apologise again, but there are only so many times you can say sorry. I took Amie by the arm and guided her on board. At least she was wearing sensible shoes but she was still tall, five seven at least, which would make her a pale-skinned Amazon amongst the women here. Despite the chill I could feel her warmth through her thin jacket as she leant against me.

'This plank really is slippery,' she said.

'I'll show you a place below where you can dry off,' I said.

'Where's Pieters?'

'Don't worry, he'll be nowhere near you.'

Twenty minutes later I took the helm of the *River Ghost* and carefully edged it out into the middle of the Ogowe. The slack was taken up from the barge rope and it followed on behind, my precious cargo of teak that had been paid for twice. Julius joined me in the cabin.

'All well with the engine, boss.'

'Good. Where's the white lady?'

'She in galley. The cook gave her eggs and coffee.'

'Okay. Take the helm now — and *concentrate*.'

I'd trained up Julius in as much navigation as he could manage. His knowledge of the river needed no help, for it was far better than mine, but he'd needed to understand what was involved in handling a boat like the *River Ghost*. He was the only black man on the river entrusted to a task like this. *Nigger lover* had been mouthed a few times behind my back at Cape Lopez, until I put a stop to it by knocking down a fat Frenchman. He'd squealed to the authorities, but I was still quite a new face here then, a war hero-cum-investor, and an asset to this burgeoning colony. The matter did not go any further.

Amie was finishing her coffee in the galley.

'Let me pour you a coffee,' she said. 'Where did you get it by the way? It's much better than anything I've drunk here so far.'

'Oh, white-devil traders have their ways.'

'Are you trying to be amusing, Mr. Hope?'

'About what?'

'The way things are here. Maybe the way things are with you? Suffering from *le grand ennui,* perhaps?'

'Are you going to treat me to a dose of café society philosophy?'

Amie smiled, the first time I'd seen her do so. It was engaging, and made her look like a young girl.

'Are you familiar with Paris?' Amie said.

'Not really. I went there a few times in the war years.'

'It's full of Americans wanting to be writers now, but most of them are really there to drink and womanise.'

'I couldn't let Pieters be run through by that chap, you know.'

'Why not? He'd have deserved it.'

'Maybe so, but I would still feel guilty.'

'And what about the man you killed? Do you feel bad about that?'

I drank my coffee and did not answer.

'Ah, you want me to change the subject. Mr. Collins told me you survived the war all the way through with barely a scratch. That's remarkable, for an officer.'

'Or any other soldier. I was lucky. I think.'

'Do I make you uncomfortable?' Amie asked, pushing back her dark hair to reveal her eyes.

There was no time to consider the question, for the boat abruptly lurched to the right. We were flung across the galley and I heard shouting everywhere.

'Are you all right?' I said.

'Yes, I think so.'

'Good. Stay here, please. I have to go.'

I dashed up on the deck of the *River Ghost*, just in time to see two mountainous shapes moving away from us in the swollen river. Hippos! Once again they had taken a dislike to my boat.

'Didn't you see them?' I yelled at Julius.

'Hard to see in rain, boss. Hippos come from under water.'

I took the wheel, wondering what else could go wrong on this trip. I soon found out. The ropes to the barge had become entangled in the collision, and the heavily-laden barge began to spin around crazily, like a giant club being wielded. The wheel was not responding to me, and Julius was shouting something in my ear.

'We all go overboard. All drown, boss.'

He was not far wrong. No one could survive in the river today. A night's downpour had turned it from placid to treacherous. A drowned man's body would soon be down on the coast and feeding the crocs there, if his bloated corpse did not get snagged up somewhere en route.

The *River Ghost* was no match for the weight of the barge. The strong wind encouraged it in its wild movements. It was pushed closer to the boat by a sudden surge of water. The logs stacked up on the barge looked very menacing. They reminded me of the giant shells of field guns.

An ashen-faced Pieters joined us on deck. He was struggling to hold onto solid things with his good arm.

'What the hell are *you* doing up here?' I shouted.

'Cut the barge loose, man!' Pieters shouted back, then followed up with something in Flemish. 'Cut it loose before this tub goes down and we all drown.'

'Okay. Take the wheel, Pieters, if you can manage it.'

'I'll manage it, even with one fucking arm.'

I took the short-handled axe from its housing in the cabin and went aft with Julius. With the blinding rain and movement of the boat it was far from easy to cut the ropes. Every time I swung the axe a rope jumped to a new position, and the rain did not help. It was almost blinding as it lashed down.

After four attempts I managed to get a heavy, direct hit and one rope parted with a loud snap. There was no need to cut through the other one because the weight of the barge was too much for a single rope. The barge broke free and the *Ghost* lurched forward again. Julius almost went overboard. I just managed to grab his jacket, which tore but held. The barge spiralled away from the *River Ghost*.

'There goes my bloody teak!' I shouted.

'You save me, boss,' Julius said.

'Never mind about that.'

Peering through the downpour, and the haze on the river that it created, I saw the detached barge start to break up as it crashed against rocks near the river banking. Teak logs started to spin away from it and head quickly towards my steamer. Now I had problems up ahead and behind.

'Julius, get two men and the dug-out poles we have in the hold.'

Julius just stared at me.

'Look, we have to push any of those logs away if they look like hitting us. And tell the boiler boys to keep shovelling. Keep steam up, for God's sake.'

Julius disappeared below but he was back on deck within a minute with two not very willing crew. They hung onto whatever they could.

I had to concentrate on what was ahead of us. A rushing swollen river would conceal many of the hazards I was familiar with, so I kept the boat in the middle of the river as far as possible. Pieters slumped in the corner of the cabin now that I had taken over the wheel.

I shouted out every curse I could think of at the thought of losing the cargo. This trip was getting better and better. One log crashed against the boat, before careering off ahead of us, I screamed at the men.

'Do your job, or we'll all be in the river!'

I was so occupied with controlling the boat that at first I didn't even realise I was shouting in English, which they did not understand. It took a few minutes wrestling with the helm as logs shot past us like sleek torpedoes. Then the river stretched out into one of its widest parts, and things settled down a little and the steering wheel was no longer fighting me for control.

The men with the poles had done a good job, pushing more than a few logs away from the *River Ghost*. I'd have to give the old boat a thorough check over at Lambaréné, but it looked like we had gotten away with it. I was back where I started, though, with no timber and very little money left.

'Get back below, Pieters,' I said. 'We're through the worst of it, and your arm is leaking. You're still losing too much blood, man. Help him down, Julius, and check the boilers. Then report back to me.'

Julius helped a very groggy Pieters back down below. He looked in a bad way now, but I wasn't sure it was because of his wound or our river adventures.

As I concentrated on keeping the *Ghost* under control, I thought of my breakfast being tossed around the galley. My empty stomach lurched in sympathy. Julius was soon back.

'All okay down below?' I said.

'Yes, boss.'

'And the French lady?'

'She in galley, talking to Pieters.' Julius offered me one of his widest smiles. 'He very white man now.'

'What's that?'

Julius' smile turned into a laugh. 'Face not red any more. He have big shock.'

I smiled too. 'Yes, big shock indeed. Take the helm again. This stretch should be smoother, but make sure you keep to the middle of the river, and watch out for those damn hippos. This rain has got them agitated.'

I went below, and Julius' description of Pieters had been accurate. He was sitting in the galley with Amie, two hands cupped around a coffee mug, his face drawn and drained of colour. He looked ten years older.

'Still in the land of the living, then?' I said.

Pieters grunted.

'I've looked at the wound,' Amie said. 'It looks like your man Julius did a fair job. I don't think it's infected, but I'm not sure.'

'You know about such things?'

'My father was a doctor, so I picked up stuff when I was younger. Sit down, Mr. Hope, there's still plenty of your fine coffee left in this pot.'

'I can sure use some.'

'I suppose I should thank you,' Pieters said, 'for what happened back in the camp. What are you going to tell the French?'

'We'll talk about that later. By the look of you, it might be a good idea to go back to your bunk.'

'Did the logs do much damage?'

'We managed to push most of them away. That was my profit going by.'

'Our profit, you mean.'

'No, *my* profit. I paid you in full last night.'

I wasn't sure whether it was an attempted smile or a grimace, but Pieters' face twisted up and all he could manage was a snort.

'Well, you got me there — *Welshman*. Okay, we'll call it quits.'

'Oh, you are not English, then?' Amie said.

'No, not at all.'

The last thing I wanted to do was talk about my antecedents. I still wasn't sure about this Frenchwoman, or what she was really doing here.

'By the way,' I said, 'what the hell is in that suitcase of yours, gold bars?'

This pricked up Pieters' interest.

'Hardly. It's my Royal typewriter. I take it everywhere.'

'Ah, for your book.'

'Maybe one day, but for now it is just articles for French magazines. You know, colonial life, how it is for French women out here, how white people behave. I'm particularly interested in that.'

She scowled at Pieters when she said this, but he was oblivious to it. In a few days the Belgian would be back to his old self, a little more cautious maybe, but none the wiser. The fact that he'd lost money over his actions would affect him much more than any moral consideration.

'I'm going to take your advice and have another lie down,' Pieters said, 'the arm hurts. Do try to keep this tub safe — *Captain*.'

He shakily got to his feet and left us.

'That man's a swine,' Amie said, 'I never did like Belgians, they're almost as bad as Germans.'

I drank my coffee. My body craved the long sleep it needed, but was not possible to have yet. At least the chef brought me some more food, which was so welcome.

'So, you are a Galois,' Amie said. 'I don't know much about Wales. It's full of coal, isn't it?'

'Something like that.'

'My mother is from Brittany. I think they are connected with Wales in some way.'

'Yes, they share a Celtic ancestry. What about your father? You said he *was* a doctor, not is.'

'He died. A shell hit his field hospital, but *Maman* is still alive and well.'

'In Paris?'

'Yes, Montmartre. She always talks about going back to the west. I know she never will, but I think she's lonely, especially now that I'm no longer with her.'

'No other children?'

'No. I'm a solitary child.'

'We say an only child.'

'That sounds better.'

'I'm one too,' I said.

'One what?'

'An only child.'

'Ah. Did you mind that?'

'I've never given it much thought.'

'I hated it. I saw the other children go home arm in arm with their siblings and was jealous. I went home to a very quiet house.'

'How is your English so good?' I said.

'Oh, that's because of my father. He was a great Anglophile. He loved everything about England and was always talking about it. He made sure I learnt the language. It's becoming the language of the world, he used to say, much to my mother's annoyance.'

'And most other French people, I should think.'

'Quite.'

Outside the slight lull in the storm ended. The rain began to lash down, and the boat became unsteady again.

'Time for me to go back on deck.'

Amie put a hand over mine as I got up.

'It must have been awful for you. Last night I mean.'

'Yes.'

'How did it feel, when you shot that man?'

The boat was rocking even more now.

'I have to go.'

With Amie's question burning in my years I took the helm from Julius just in time. Up ahead the river diverged into three sections, but the storm and excess water would make precise navigation crucial.

'Keep the stokers busy below,' I said. 'We're losing steam again.'

It was an intense fifteen minutes, but we got through this choppy stretch of the river intact. The Ogowe now stretched out before me in a much flatter expanse that was not greatly affected by the floodwaters coming down from the interior. We would be in Lambaréné by early evening.

So intent was I on steering the boat I did not notice that Amie had appeared on deck. She came into the bridge with a makeshift sandwich, a piece of fried chicken wedged between two chunks of the chef's stale bread, plus a mug of coffee she had somehow managed not to spill

'I thought you might need this,' she said.

'Where did the chicken come from?'

'I brought some with me, a gift from Ann Collins.'

'Thank you, it's very welcome, but you shouldn't be on deck. We're not safe yet.'

'Your Mr. Pieters seems better. I think he's looking for what's left of your rum.'

'He's certainly not *my* Mr. Pieters, and Musbewi has had all the booze. That's a pity, because an inebriated Pieters toppling overboard would be very welcome.'

*

With Sebastian on his lap, Schweitzer was having his usual pre-surgery pipe on the veranda when Gillespie arrived. The young man waved up to Schweitzer as his dugout glided to a halt. Schweitzer waved back. He hurried down to the riverbank, scattering a few hens as he did so. They clucked around his feet, but stood their ground when the cat came close.

Schweitzer shook the young man's hand like it was a village pump from back home. The men in the dugout grinned at this rare animated display from the white *oganga*, especially as it was starting to rain again.

'You should have stayed in the dry, Doctor,' Gillespie said. 'You're getting wet.'

'No more than you, my boy. Come, back to the house. We have some good coffee now, courtesy of Mr. Hope. No doubt you could do with a hot breakfast too.'

'I certainly could.'

'I did not expect you until this afternoon. You must have been on the river through the night.'

'Yes.'

'Was that wise? The Ogowe is difficult enough in daylight, and hippos can be nocturnal, you know.'

'I trust the men in the dugout. It's their world after all, and we did have a small lantern.'

'Yes, their world indeed.'

They hurried back up the slope to Schweitzer's house.

'I wanted to get back down as soon as possible,' Gillespie said, 'before Hope arrived.'

'Oh?'

'Yes, I have news, Doctor, very bad news.'

Gillespie quickly related what he'd been told about the shooting.

'I knew that man would be trouble,' Gillespie said, as he finished his report.

Schweitzer sighed, and sucked vigorously on his re-filled pipe.

'Are you sure all this is accurate?' Schweitzer asked.

'I am, Doctor.'

Schweitzer sat down heavily and looked at the floor as he spoke. He felt a great need to play the piano.

'I've always thought that *Thou Shalt Not Kill* is very much the strongest of all the Commandments,' Schweitzer said. 'It's also the one that the world has spectacularly failed to keep, in my lifetime or any other time. It especially troubles me that so often religion and carnage seem to go hand in hand, but I've never made the mistake of blaming my faith for it.'

'But there does seems no end to it,' Gillespie said. 'Quite the opposite, in fact.'

'It is human weakness, but I think a weakness that God himself has installed in us. He gives us the chance to engage with it, conquer it, and then become stronger in the belief.'

Gillespie was silent for a long moment.

'I know you are beset by doubts,' Schweitzer said. 'I was at your age, but this is still my creed. I've tried to use it as an argument whenever I've come up against atheists. Those who say there is no god, for how can there be when the world is so stubbornly murderous and cruel? When so many creatures kill to survive, man most of all? Darwinism has reinforced their argument, and what man of intelligence could deny a survival-of-the-fittest regime when walking through the land here? The strong prey on the weak.'

'Hope is probably an atheist,' Gillespie muttered.

'He has not said that to me. We should wait until we hear what he has to say about this business before we judge. It seems that this man Pieters was the cause of this tragedy. That does not surprise me.'

Schweitzer felt despair at the news. Adam Hope had intrigued him, and, he realised now, he had also taken to the man, even though Hope was someone totally alien to his world. He was a man of war, action and commerce, but he thought there was an honesty and integrity about him that shone through, plus of course the pain. It permeated that young man's character, like an enduring smoke that could not be dissipated. This made him a mystery, and Schweitzer had hoped to help him. Now Hope had killed a man, not far from Lambaréné.

'You should get some sleep now,' Schweitzer said.

'Don't you need me in the surgery?'

'Not today. A medical student out on his feet with tiredness would be dangerous. Go to bed, Noel, and we'll talk later.'

'Hope will be here by then.'

'Yes, I know.'

Schweitzer sat deep in thought until he was called to surgery. It would not be too busy a day for him. He had planned to go through his notes for his latest book in the next few weeks, and also to oversee the ongoing work required at Lambaréné, but the news about Hope changed things.

The hospital refurbishment was slowly taking shape, but slow was the right word. The strong work ethic that had been instilled in Schweitzer from a very early age was often not present in others. He was always cajoling, berating, and sometimes even begging the men here to work in the way that had been agreed, but what the white man had brought did not help. His workers sought after rum and tobacco, and when they got it work often came to a full stop.

Schweitzer had quickly grown fond of Gillespie, and the young Oxford man had a history that intrigued him. When Gillespie's mother had lived in Syria she had met T.E. Lawrence, then a young archaeologist. Lawrence had guided Gillespie's childhood reading. Although borne out of war, the story, or perhaps legend, of Lawrence of Arabia had fascinated Schweitzer when it became well known. He thought there was something almost biblical about it. It was certainly stirring that one man could achieve so much.

Schweitzer pulled at his moustache and scolded himself for the vanity of thinking that one day he might be Schweitzer of Africa. For a moment he let his mind wander. He thought of the great explorers who had come before him, men like Livingstone, Burton, and many others. Some of them would have been godly men, others certainly not, but they were all men of vision, and he empathised with that. He finished Hope's coffee, and wondered how that troubled young man would be feeling now.

*

We arrived at Lambaréné at midday. I had to bring the boat downriver at the slowest speed possible, just in case more damage had been done than first thought. I moored the *River Ghost* as close to the bank at Lambaréné as I dared. This time there were no excited locals to greet us. The unrelenting rain kept them indoors.

'Make sure Pieters stays here,' I told Julius, 'if he wakes up, that is. I'm taking the lady up to the doctor's house.'

I ushered Amie on ahead as I struggled with her suitcase, and wondered how she ever managed it herself. I thought it would have made sense for her to write longhand rather than suffer such a weight-lifting chore, then type it all up when she got back to civilisation.

Amie was the first writer I'd ever met, if you discounted war correspondents and poets, and most of them had been drunk when I had been obliged to talk to them. Amie was obviously quite proud of her 'little Royal,' as she put it. I remembered the great iron beasts in my father's shipping office, which would have taken a few local porters to heft around.

Schweitzer was on his veranda to meet us.

'Ah, Mr. Hope, you are back.'

As Amie stepped up onto the veranda the doctor stretched out a hand to her, and when she offered hers he kissed it in quite a showy way. I was surprised that the missionary had such a romantic side, but then I barely knew the man.

'You must be Amie Moreau,' Schweitzer said. 'My assistant here, Mr. Gillespie, has told me about you. You met him upriver.'

'Indeed,' Amie said, 'and it's such an honour to meet you at last, Dr. Schweitzer. You are getting quite famous, you know.'

'Oh, I hardly think so, young lady, but do come in. Come in out of the rain, both of you.'

'Is Gillespie back with you?' I asked.

'Yes, he is. He arrived early this morning.'

I knew that Schweitzer was aware of the killing as soon as he said this, but Amie's presence stilled his tongue, for now.

'I have a room here where you could have some privacy,' Schweitzer said to Amie. 'You need to put on dry clothes. It's easy to get a chill in these conditions, and chills here can lead to more serious things. I know this only too well.'

'Thank you, Doctor.'

Schweitzer escorted Amie away, leaving me feeling awkward, as if waiting for the headmaster outside his study in my dreadful school days.

'I've put the young lady in Helene's sanctuary,' Schweitzer said when he returned. 'It was a place where my wife could be apart from the toil of Lambaréné, when it got too much.'

The doctor seemed lost in his thoughts for a moment.

'You *have* been told what happened in Musbewi's camp, haven't you?' I said.

'Yes, Gillespie has told me. It's a terrible business, Mr. Hope.'

'Yes.'

'Come into my study. You look exhausted.'

'It's been one hell of a night. Oh, I'm sorry, Doctor.'

'No, that's quite all right. Hell might be an apt description for it.'

Schweitzer offered me his armchair whilst he went to a cupboard, from where, to my amazement, he produced a bottle of spirits.

'I was sent this fine whisky by a well wisher,' he said. 'Yes, a well wisher who does not know me very well, because I'm, how you say, a tee—?'

'Tee-totaller?'

'Yes, that's it. English is so rich in such terms. The bottle has never been opened, not even for medicinal purposes, but I think you could use some. I thought to offer you some when you were first here with Mr. Pieters, but knew that would be unwise.'

Schweitzer found a glass from a collection of them on a small tray in the corner, and carefully poured out a liberal measure.

'Is this enough?' he said, 'it's not something I've done of much before.'

'Yes. It's much appreciated.'

It was hard to keep my hand steady as I took the glass. I sipped the fine old whisky, savouring it by moving it around my mouth and letting it warm my palate before swallowing.

'So please tell me what happened, all of it,' Schweitzer said.

We talked for fifteen minutes, but it seemed much longer than that for me.

'Pieters is indeed a sinner,' Schweitzer said, 'and sinners always draw others into their misdeeds. And a poor man has died because of it.'

'I've been over it so many times in my head. I'm doing so now.'

'No doubt it has brought back your war experiences. You must have seen so much suffering.'

'I'm no different to millions of others, except that I'm still alive.'

Schweitzer got up and stood by the window.

'The rain is strengthening again. We'll have two solid weeks of it now.'

'Are you expecting the *Alemba* soon?'

'Yes, probably tomorrow. Captain Penaud usually arrives at the start of the wet season.'

'Yes, he does.'

'Everything happens for a reason,' Schweitzer said. 'That's always been one of my mantras, and we are all slaves to our destinies, in one way or another — that's another.'

'I should have watched Pieters more closely in Musbewi's camp. If I had I would have prevented what happened.'

'Hindsight is a cruel master. From what I have been told, you did what you had to do to save Pieters. It was that man's

113

desire to take a life that caused the loss of his own. It was ever thus, I fear.'

Each of us sank into silence, Schweitzer pulling at his moustache, until Joseph broke in on our thoughts. He was calling out to the doctor, and then entered the room, with Julius alongside him.

'I told you to stay with the boat,' I said.

'What is it, Joseph?' Schweitzer said, but it was Julius who answered.

'Boss, Pieters man very sick again. He shouts and go crazy in his bunk. I think he got big fever now. He all hot.'

'Joseph, bring him up to the surgery,' Schweitzer said. 'Go with Mr. Hope's man.'

'Pieters is nothing but trouble,' I muttered.

'Yes, the worst of us usually are. I'll prepare the surgery to receive him. Gillespie is already there. This will be good training for him. Please rest in the armchair. You need it.'

Schweitzer was right about that. I still did not know what he really thought about me, and I realised that to know that was important to me.

*

Schweitzer knew that Pieters was in trouble as soon as he saw the arm. Pieters was barely conscious when he was helped into the surgery. The wound in his arm looked very ugly.

'It's badly infected,' Schweitzer said. 'It can happen so quickly here. Look, you can practically see the disease making its way up the man's arm. Well, what's your diagnosis, Mr. Gillespie?'

'Could gangrene have set in so soon?'

'Yes it could, and it has. Well done, young man.'

Schweitzer wafted a hand as he bent his head closer to the wound.

'The putrefaction of living flesh is foul indeed,' he murmured. 'We have no time to lose, or this man will be dead within forty-eight hours, maybe sooner, and it will be a miserable death at that.'

'This is the man involved in the business upriver, I take it?'

'The very same.' Schweitzer pulled at his moustache, twirling it around with his fingers. 'The Lord does work in mysterious ways. Adam Hope takes a life, and then maybe saves one by bringing this man to us.'

'Are we talking amputation here, Doctor?'

'We are, otherwise the poison will be in his blood stream, and I'll have no way of saving him then.'

Schweitzer issued rapid orders to Joseph, who got the necessary equipment together.

'Have you carried out an amputation before, Noel?'

'No, but I've sent a few.'

So intense was Gillespie's concentration that it took him a moment to realise that Schweitzer had now used his Christian name for the second time. He rather liked it.

'So, would you like to do the procedure yourself?' Schweitzer said. 'I think you are ready, and we all have to start somewhere. Don't worry, I will be right here alongside you. I have done many removals of limbs, too many, for there are so many dangers for people in the forests here. I will act as your anaesthetist.'

Gillespie was very nervous. As Schweitzer applied the ether to Pieters, he took up the saw. He hoped that his hand would not shake too much.

*

It was a strange dream, even by my standards. Images of early childhood clashed with violent scenes from the war. One second I was on a beach with my mother, looking on enviously as large groups of children played together, then it was over the top for Lucky Hope. Head down into hell, shoulders hunched, blowing that stupid whistle so that my men could follow me like sheep. They were more like lambs to the slaughter.

I should have been the first man down. Junior officers usually were, shot or blown up in their droves to be buried alongside the other ranks, an equality in death that had never been known in the army before. In that war the numbers were so vast it was the only way.

I could smell that beach, the brine in the air, and hear the excited voices all around me, but at seven years old I was required to sit sedately with my mother. My father was not with us. He very rarely was, which I thought a blessing in those early days.

Now I'm back in my bunk in the officers' dugout again, trying to sleep amidst an assortment of pungent smells, praying that my batman won't tug me awake again. He was an odd but attentive little chap called Hicks. It's a fond hope because he *is* trying to wake me, his polite but insistent hand is pulling at my shoulder. Wake up, sir, wake up.

My eyes opened, but it's Amie Moreau I saw, not Corporal Hicks. She was inches from my face, and for a moment I was not sure if this was another part of the dream. Her dark eyes gaze intently into mine.

'You have been in a deep sleep for hours. The doctor thought it better not to wake you.'

I got up slowly.

'What time is it?'

'About midday.'

I rubbed the sleep from my eyes as my stomach let me know how empty it was.

'Where's Dr. Schweitzer?'

'He is just finishing up his surgery. He's been busy with Pieters.'

'I must have gone out like a light.'

'Like a light?'

'Just an English expression.'

'Ah. We say *s'endormir en un clin d'oeil*.'

'I'll remember that. It sounds much more elegant.'

'I have prepared some late breakfast for you.'

'*You* have?'

'Yes, the doctor is very kind. He said that I could have the run of the kitchen here. His usual man is helping in the surgery.'

I followed Amie into the kitchen, noticing the undulation of her hips as she moved. She had changed her clothing, and was wearing a simple cream dress that I found quite alluring. Perhaps I *was* still dreaming after all.

Schweitzer's kitchen was a lean-to affair at the side of the house. It had a corrugated metal roof and was not very inviting, but as soon as I smelt the coffee brewing there I loved the place.

Amie watched me eat the simple meal she had prepared without saying much. I got the feeling that she was not a talkative woman, and that suited me.

'You are very quiet,' Amie finally said.

'We both are.'

'Do you like Dr. Schweitzer?'

'Well, I certainly admire what he's trying to do here.'

'Indeed — the white man bringing gifts.'

'What do you mean by that?'

'Schweitzer seems to be building a little empire here. *Le Grand Patron*, you might say.'

'Do you see something wrong in what he's doing at Lambaréné?'

'Not wrong, but have you noticed the way he treats his staff? The black ones, that is? It's like he's the father figure that always knows best. People have lived in Africa much longer than we have in Europe, and I'm sure they always managed without our so-called help.'

'Is that what you're writing about? The white man's intrusion into Africa?'

'Invasion might be a better word.'

'Maybe so, but nothing is going to change that any time soon. Africa is complicated, and will be for a long time to come, in my opinion. And don't forget, Schweitzer is a Victorian. He comes from a very different background to us.'

'I know, but times are changing back home, in France anyway. Maybe even in England. I'm told it's all American jazz and suffragettes over there now.'

'In London, yes, but I'm afraid all that has passed me by, what with the war and coming out here.'

'I love jazz, myself. I danced to it in Paris. It made me feel so free, so different to the way that I was brought up. And being here now makes me think how wonderful it is that black people are bringing us a new art form, and how ironic too.'

'Ironic?'

'Yes, because with jazz they are the masters and we the pupils.'

I had an image of Amie swirling around in smoky Parisian basements, watched by the eager eyes of many men.

'It enrages my mother that I love it so,' Amie continued, 'but that makes it even more attractive to me.'

'Aren't parents supposed to be alarmed when their children find new things, new ways?'

Schweitzer joined us.

'How's Pieters?' I said.

'Mlle Moreau has not told you? I'm afraid that he is now minus an arm.'

'Good God. You had to amputate?'

'Yes, the spear wound had become too badly infected. The gangrene would have killed him.'

'Does he know about it yet? Is he alert?'

'Not yet, but he soon will be.'

An arm for a life, I thought. That was a better result than usual for the people here, but I knew it would hit Pieters hard. His drinking would increase, if that was possible, and his future was bleak.

'Let me get you some coffee, Doctor,' Amie said. 'You probably need it.'

'Thank you, but I did not amputate the arm myself. That was the job of Mr. Gillespie. It was his first such operation and he did very well. He'll be joining us shortly. He's looking forward to meeting you, Mr. Hope.'

We sat down at a sturdy but worm-eaten table and there was an awkward silence for a while. Schweitzer seemed not to notice, and was obviously enjoying his coffee. I doubted that Gillespie was looking forward to meeting me at all. My presence here made things difficult for everyone.

I felt like leaving Lambaréné quickly, but my men were spooked by what had happened, so a few days' rest and food in safe surroundings would do them the world of good.

Gillespie joined us. He was quite young, at least three or four years younger than I was. I got up and shook the hand that was hesitantly offered.

'So you are Adam Hope?' Gillespie said.

I nodded.

'Pieters will survive then?' I said.

'There is no reason why he shouldn't,' Schweitzer said, 'as long as he keeps the wound clean.'

'That might be difficult, the type of man he is.'

'I agree, so I think it would be better that he stays here. When the *Alemba* comes back he can go back with Captain Penaud to Cape Lopez. By then he should be out of danger.'

'That will be a great imposition for you, Doctor.'

'Lambaréné is used to such things. Medical emergencies are just that — emergencies. Besides, it will be a big shock to Pieters when he realises he has lost an arm. He will need time to come to terms with it.'

'Not that Lambaréné is used to accommodating people who have been involved in a shooting,' Gillespie said.

'No, I shouldn't think it is,' I said. 'It happened so quickly, but things like that usually do.'

'I'd hardly call the death of another human being a *thing,* particularly as the incident was caused by Pieters' disgusting behaviour.'

'This is a violent land, Mr. Gillespie. I'm sure the doctor could tell you of the many spear, knife, and machete wounds he has dealt with over the years.'

'I see you are a cynic, Mr. Hope,' Gillespie said.

'A pragmatist maybe, but I don't think I'm a cynic. And I know this country rather better than you, Gillespie.'

Schweitzer held up a hand.

'Gentlemen, we have a young lady present. This is not the time to discuss such matters, and Noel, you need to rest after your work today. I can well remember my first amputation, and how exhausted I felt afterwards. You did a good job, by the way.'

'Very well, sir.' Gillespie touched an imaginary hat to Amie as he left the room. 'I bid you good day, Madame.'

'I'm not a madame,' Amie mouthed to herself. 'English people always get that wrong.'

'I too have to leave you,' Schweitzer said. 'Dealing with Pieters means that my regular surgery work has been delayed. We'll have people arriving now who will need our help, trudging through the rains like the lost souls they are.'

'Oh I wouldn't say they are lost souls at all, Doctor,' Amie said. 'Hurt and sick, certainly, but not lost. I think most people here know exactly who they are. They are vibrant, and at one with nature. They have something that we lost a long time ago.'

Schweitzer smiled. 'Maybe we can discuss this later.'

The doctor left us, closing the door much more quietly that Gillespie had.

'Was I rude then?' Amie said.

'There's nothing wrong in speaking your mind.'

'There is if you're a woman, especially out here. I found that out at Cape Lopez. I was introduced to all the leading colonials there. They were all old-school French, and twenty years behind the times. People trying to recreate the lives they once had back home, lives from before the war. That was a time when women were required only to be decorative, and not to talk about important matters.'

'Well you're certainly not one of them.'

Amie smiled. 'More coffee, Monsieur?'

*

Schweitzer sat on the front step of the house, smoking his pipe and fondling the head of Sebastian. The cat kept just out of range of the tobacco smoke. This was Schweitzer's main thinking spot. A violent death close to Lambaréné gave him plenty to reflect on, especially when the man who had killed was under his roof.

As usual, he exhaled his pipe smoke upwards. It was a habit he'd perfected to keep the flies away. It soon formed a defensive cloud that he knew they detested. Helene had tolerated his addiction but he knew she thought it filthy. At least his foul smoke would not affect his daughter as she grew up. He felt a sudden stab of longing to see Rhena, and smoked even harder.

Schweitzer's thoughts began to fixate on the shooting again. He did not doubt Hope's account of what had happened in Musbewi's camp. The man Pieters had a very dissolute air about him. Men like him were not rare in this colony.

The rain had stopped during the amputation of Pieters' arm, but Schweitzer knew that when the first drops started to fall again it would turn into a deluge in seconds. That was the way of life here. Slow moving, almost trance-like days in the sun, then an explosion of nature in all its power.

Sometimes he thought Gabon must be one of God's favourite places, such was the diversity he had invested in it. The people here had long adjusted to the weather. They were often indolent in the most exasperating ways, and then they too seemed to explode, with industry, ingenuity, and sometimes rage. Did this make them closer to nature, in a way most white men had lost? Maybe. Amie Moreau certainly thought so.

Schweitzer still had not made his mind up about Hope. He needed more time, and there were so many demands on that. He had to manage numerous strands of his life at Lambaréné. There was the rebuilding project, his medical duties, his theological and philosophical writings, and the charting of his work here in book form. The latter had been a welcome distraction, and a lucrative surprise. Now he was thinking ahead to his next book.

Helene had sent him an article from a Paris newspaper in which he had been called a polymath. He was, but sometimes he wished that his interests were less far ranging. He'd gone from Jesus to Bach, but many other interests had been sandwiched in between. All roads had eventually led him to Lambaréné, and he knew now, in his heart of hearts, that here he would stay. To think he was on his personal road to Damascus would be foolish vanity, but he did feel God had called him, and was guiding him.

Some years ago Schweitzer had read a book by the American author Mark Twain, in which Twain said there are two important days in one's life, the day you are born and the day you realise why. He thought that profound, and that second day had brought him to Lambaréné.

Schweitzer finished his pipe and went back into the house. He looked into the main living room to see the Frenchwoman curled up on the old Ottoman he had there. Her body was crumpled with tiredness, and to him she still looked like a child. Perhaps she too was looking for her life to be given meaning in Africa. Everyone was searching for something.

Gillespie knocked lightly on the door and entered.

'You don't have to knock, Noel.'

'I find it hard to get out of the habit, Doctor.'

'What is it?'

'The Belgian has woken up, and he is not happy.'

*

I was up early next morning, taking advantage of a few dry hours to stretch my legs around Lambaréné. I'd lain awake most of the night in my bunk, listening to the nightlife as I went over every second of the shooting in my head. I could have left Pieters to his fate, and a big part of me wished to hell that I had. If the situation were reversed, would I have shot the Belgian to save the spearman? That was a question that went around and around in my head like a whirlpool on the Ogowe, but without resolution.

The jungle was between downpours, and thick growth was heavy with water. It dripped constantly from bush and tree, and the ground underfoot was soggy. It was easy to sink your boots into mud if not careful.

Amie was so well camouflaged I did not see her at first. She was wearing a light green dress that blended in with the foliage behind her. She called out to me.

'Hello, Hope,' she said, her voice barely rising above the insect chorus.

'Hello yourself. You really shouldn't be this far from the main buildings.'

'Schweitzer's house is only a few hundred metres away.'

'That's far enough for anything to happen in the jungle. There are leopards around, you know, and snakes of all varieties. Some of them can kill you.'

Amie shrugged, a Gallic gesture if ever I saw one.

'I walked quite a lot when I was in Musbewi's camp, and I'm still here. I can look after myself. I just wanted to get away for a while and smoke a cigarette on my own. I don't think the doctor is used to young women smoking, I think it unnerves him slightly.'

Now that I had got closer I could see a thin film of sweat on Amie's upper lip. I instinctively brushed back my hair, which was at its unkempt best.

'Well, if you walk closer to the hospital I'll let you be, if that is what you want.'

'You are here now. You can be my guard, from these *awful* dangers.'

Amie took a small cigarette case from a pocket that was concealed in her dress.

'Do you want one?' she asked.

'I'm more of a cigar man myself, but okay, I will, thanks. Are they French?'

'Of course. Gitanes are all I ever smoke. I'm running low now, though. Only one packet left after these.'

'Same here with cigars. I'm down to smoking the ones I sell, and that's a very sad state of affairs.'

'Well some might say — how do you say it in English — rough—?'

'Rough justice. *Touché*. And do *you* say that?'

'I don't know enough about you yet.'

'You know I've killed a man.'

'Yes, but Schweitzer still seems to like you. That surprises me.'

'Yes, me too. But all great men are complicated, aren't they?'

'Not just great men,' Amie murmured.

Amie lit her cigarette with a lighter that matched the case. When she offered me the flame I cupped my hands around it to protect it from the breeze, and held her hand still for a moment. It was warm and moist, and she didn't pull it away after I'd lit the cigarette. Amie offered me another thin smile. I was getting used to them now.

The French cigarette felt tiny in my fingers. They were more used to the fat butts of cigars, but it was a good smoke. Cigarettes and whisky had been the staple diet of officers in the war, and I now had a lifetime's addiction to both.

'Is Schweitzer a part of your writing plans then?' I said.

Another shrug came.

'He's quite famous in Paris, you know,' Amie said. 'My parents took me to see one of his organ recitals once. They loved it.'

'And you?'

'Not really. Music like that is part of a society I am trying to escape.'

'Another one on the run, eh? Hence that new jazz stuff?'

'It's not stuff, it's an art form, and I'm not on the run. I think *you* are though, Hope.'

'I think it's time you called me Adam.'

'Okay, but what kind of name is Hope anyway?'

'It's the one I come with.'

We walked on for a while, until we came to a good spot to sit, a log that had been left to weather for many years, by the look of it. The Ogowe was at one of its wider points at Lambaréné. It stretched away from us, a fat river swollen with rainwater and debris that the storms had dislodged from the river's banks. In the distance beyond the river a fringe of blue hills loomed out of a menacing sky. Another storm was imminent, but at the moment all was still and calm.

'The weather is so strange here,' Amie said. 'It was warm and humid earlier; now it's feeling fresh again.'

'Yes, that's because it's about to rain once more. Enjoy it whilst you can, because once the rains are over the heat will return with a vengeance. How long have you been here, Amie?

'In Africa, you mean?'

'Yes.'

'I left Marseilles about two months ago.'

'And you've lugged that typewriter around all that time?'

'Lugged?'

'Carried.'

'Of course, although I usually get a big, strong man like you to help me, if I can.'

Before I could even react to her teasing Amie leant forward and kissed me. I returned it, and this close she smelt of mint tea and a perfume I could not name.

'That was unexpected,' I said.

'The best kisses always are.'

She leant even closer to me.

'Has it been a long time?' she said.

'Long enough.'

'Has there been anyone before, anyone serious, I mean?'

'Only one, and that was a long time ago. In another world, you might say. What about you?'

'Not really, not anyone special anyway. Plenty of ships passing by in the night, though.'

'You are very frank, Amie. People back home would say forward.'

'Yes, in Paris too, but we are not back home.'

'No.'

Amie pushed herself firmly against my chest now. I could feel the outline of her slim, lithe figure and her small breasts that pressed into me. She played with my shirt buttons with one hand, and my hair with the other.

'Adam.' She mouthed my name a few times, her mouth not straying far from mine. 'Adam — the first man. I like that. How long will you stay at Lambaréné, Adam the first man?'

'I'm not sure. The *River Ghost* was pretty banged up on that trip down, and I will have to talk to Captain Penaud when he arrives with the *Alemba*. I'm not at all sure how that is going to go.'

'Penaud? Don't worry about him. I can wrap him around my little finger.'

'You know him, then? *He's* not one of your passing ships, is he?'

Amie laughed, a light, airy sound that made me even more attracted to her.

'Don't be silly. Penaud reminds me of my father, and that is *not* a good thought.'

We kissed again, until a few local men disturbed us. They were noisily making their way through the undergrowth, which was fortunate for us, otherwise they'd by running to the doctor with their great tale.

'Have I confused you?' Amie said, as we sat apart again. 'Maybe frightened you a little?'

'Only one person frightens me, and he exists only in a dream. Come on, we'd better be getting back.'

As soon as we neared the hospital, and the people working around it, Amie linked arms with mine. I couldn't stop her.

'Why not?' she said, 'we're adults, aren't we?'

*

Schweitzer saw Hope and Amie coming. He was taking a few minutes of air after a difficult surgery. More patients were arriving daily, for the rains stopped much of the work in the forest. Today he'd dealt with skin lesions, snakebites, and one woman who was convinced evil spirits possessed her. She had writhed around until he had managed to calm her down. This was another new skill he had learned at Lambaréné, but it was draining work. Schweitzer also had other concerns when the rains came, for his workers would often melt away for a few weeks, some never to return.

Hope and the Frenchwoman made a fine couple, Schweitzer thought, if that was what they now were. As they strode towards him he realised how kind nature had been to them. They were handsome, healthy, tall and clean limbed, such opposites to most of his patients. But he knew that Adam Hope was only like this on the outside. Schweitzer had seen enough of him now to know that there was turmoil inside that man. His was a soul wracked by pain and guilt, a young man still traumatised by the war. He'd known this before this awful business upriver. Now that Hope had killed again all his old wounds would open up, to say nothing about a life tragically taken. These were not wounds that any surgeon could heal.

The killing of the man in Musbewi's camp troubled Schweitzer very much. He had prayed for that lost soul last night, and he had also prayed for Hope. Violent death had never been this close to him before. He had been shielded from it in the war, but so many of his friends on both sides had perished. His time in internment with Helene had been hard, and each of them had suffered illness, but that could never compare to the horrors of the war.

Schweitzer still felt some unease about his easier path. So many millions had died whilst he'd sat out the war in safety. But years before the conflict started he had already found his main purpose in life. God had shown him his road and he had walked down it. The reason for his life was all around him at Lambaréné, in his patients, in the land, and the life that teemed everywhere here. He knew this was at his core, for he had a reverence for life, life in all its forms.

Schweitzer looked at his pocket watch. It was two in the afternoon and the *Alemba* was expected in a few hours. He looked forward to it, for Captain Penaud was good company, and he liked Bach. That was a bonus in these rapidly changing times. Penaud usually expected an impromptu concert, and Schweitzer was not averse to that. If he was honest he rather liked showing off his skills.

Schweitzer acknowledged the approaching pair with a wave of his hand, but as he prepared to meet them Joseph appeared on the veranda. He was disturbed, which was not that unusual for him.

'Come quick, sir,' Joseph shouted. 'Pieters man is calling for you, saying bad things.'

'Calm yourself, Joseph. I'm coming. Mr. Hope and Mademoiselle are approaching. See that you offer them refreshments.'

Schweitzer made his way to the hospital, where Pieters had been placed in a side room. As soon as he saw the Belgian Schweitzer knew that reality had hit home. Pieters was propped up in bed, his face shiny with sweat. It had also soaked through the thin bedclothes and his face was pale and drawn, with bristles sprouting all over it in black smudges.

'Why did you take my fucking arm?' Pieters shouted. 'What good is a one-armed man out here? What good is he anywhere?'

'Please don't blaspheme here, Mr. Pieters. I understand your rage, but your own actions caused this. You must learn to live with it, but you are still the master of your own fate.'

'What the hell are you talking about?'

'Your poor behaviour caused your wound and the subsequent loss of your arm, and more importantly it cost the life of another human being. If we hadn't taken it off you would have died. Infection had taken hold. Another few hours and it would have been all through your body.'

'Maybe it would have been better if I *had* died.'

'Life is too precious to dismiss like that. We should hold onto it, revere it, until our race is done. You are not thinking straight at the moment.'

'Don't give me any of your God-squad claptrap.'

'What I *can* give you is a sedative to ease your trauma. As for the surgery, it went well. As long as the wound is kept clean you will heal.'

Pieters beat the bed with his one arm in frustration.

'Careful, you'll disturb your dressing.'

'But what can I do, Doctor? I can't work with one arm. You tell me — what can I do?'

'Tens of thousands of men came home from the war like you, and many were far worse off, but they will survive. You too will survive, and whilst you heal perhaps you'll have time to reflect on your past life.'

Pieters became quiet, and let Schweitzer administer the sedative. For now he was done. He didn't want to say more, but his mind was becoming alive with all sorts of thoughts.

*

I was not sure if Amie was stalking me, whether she was a woman who had identified her prey and was moving in on it. Maybe I was to be another ship in the night. I needed time to clear my head but Amie pressed close to me again and stared intently up at my face.

'I'd love to know what you're thinking right now,' she said.

We had reached Schweitzer's veranda, where a few roughly hewn wooden chairs had been placed. There was a black and white cat on one, but Amie swept it off. The doctor seemed to have disappeared.

'Let's sit here,' Amie said. 'It's a good place to catch the breeze.'

She lit up another of her cigarettes but this time I didn't want one. They were too small in my hands and they did not last long enough for me.

'So what are you thinking, Adam Hope?'

'About what?'

'Oh, about life. Anything you want. About me?'

I took a moment. The sky over the far hills was getting angry again, and dark blue clouds were edged with a deeper black. They rose up majestically on the horizon, and there was a distant roll of thunder, like faraway drums.

'It looks like it's going to be heavy,' Amie said, nodding into the distance. 'What do they say about it in English, something about cats?'

'Raining cats and dogs.'

'Ah yes. You haven't answered my question, Adam.'

'It's been a long time since I had a conversation this intimate.'

'So?'

'I think before we talk about any future, I need to sort out what happened up river. Penaud will be here soon.'

'The future? *Our* future? Aren't you are getting ahead of yourself.'

'Am I?'

Amie pressed a hand down on one of mine. She almost burned me with her cigarette, but the ash that fell was nearly spent.

'I'm not talking about any future,' Amie said, 'I'm talking about the here and now. It's far more important. People spend so much time looking back, or ahead, that they lose a great deal of the present. After surviving that damned war I would have thought you'd have realised that.'

Amie finished her cigarette as she waited for me to say something, crushing the butt under her foot, without any respect for Schweitzer's environment.

'Let me make it easier for you,' Amie said. She leant forward and kissed me. It took me by surprise but I responded. For some crazy reason my father came into my head. I saw him clearly, calling Amie a loose woman and a foreign one at that, puffed up with fake anger to hide his jealousy. It made Amie seem even more attractive to me. We kissed again, just as Schweitzer re-appeared, warning us with a discreet cough. Amie giggled.

'Mr. Pieters was very agitated,' Schweitzer said. 'I gave him something to make him sleep. I'm afraid he's taken it very hard.'

'Who wouldn't?' I said.

'You should have let that man run him through with the spear,' Amie said. 'It would have been easier for everyone.'

'Violence is never the answer,' Schweitzer said.

That man was running at me again. He was a figure down all the ages, a man with a spear, a weapon of choice since history had been recorded, and no doubt for millennia before that. I could still see the intent in his eyes. All reason had been crowded out of him by anger, and the need to feed it. Fix it. Eyes like that had lived alongside me all through the war. No doubt he would join the German boy in my nightmares. At this moment I felt like going to Pieters and pressing a pillow down on the bastard's face.

Joseph appeared with a tray of drinks.

'Thank you, Joseph,' Schweitzer said, 'you can join Mr. Gillespie now for the rest of surgery. We have three more patients that need our attention.'

The next storm duly arrived, just as Schweitzer served the tea, and Amie was right, it was a bad one. Rain swept up to the veranda in a solid sheet of water, moving us quickly inside.

We settled down in Schweitzer's main room. I felt very uncomfortable, but Amie seemed quite relaxed. It was hard to tell what Schweitzer was thinking. His expression never changed much. There was a kind of inscrutability about the man.

Amie talked in French with Schweitzer about mundane things, but her eyes were always on me. I was glad when we heard a series of sharp toots coming up from the river. It just about carried over the noise of the downpour. The *Alemba* was arriving.

'Ah, it's Captain Penaud,' Schweitzer said, 'getting here just as the storm is raging. How typical of the man.'

Only a few of the Lambaréné locals ventured out into the storm to greet the boat. There was none of the usual buzz of excited action, for the rain ruled today. Besides being captain of the *Alemba*, Penaud was used by the French as a kind of riverboat policeman here.

Ten minutes later the squat figure of Penaud loomed out of the grey mist the rain had created. He was trying to shelter under a large black umbrella that the wind was trying to blow away from him. He was soaked through by the time he stepped up onto the veranda, where he stood in his own puddle, stamping his feet until Schweitzer invited him in.

'It's good to be back,' Penaud said, 'and always an honour to see you, Doctor.'

'You should have stayed on board the *Alemba* until the rain eased,' Schweitzer said.

'Time waits for no man. Isn't that right, Mr. Hope?'

Penaud thrust out a hand that I was obliged to take. For a moment I expected handcuffs to appear. Penaud noticed Amie, who was sitting furthest from the door.

'Why, Mademoiselle Moreau. We meet again. This *is* an unexpected pleasure.'

Penaud made a show of kissing Amie's hand.

'I was hoping you'd be here,' Penaud said to me, 'and Pieters also?'

'Yes. So you *do* know, then?' I said.

'Two of Musbewi's men met the *Alemba* when we were a day out of Cape Lopez. They must have come down the river in record time. Until we managed to calm them down I thought a tribal war had broken out. I'm glad Pieters is here. I suspected he might have disappeared into the interior, a man like that.'

'He's in no state to go anywhere,' Schweitzer said. 'He's lost an arm.'

'Has he indeed? Well I suppose there's a kind of justice in that.'

'Joseph is busy helping Gillespie,' Schweitzer said, 'but soon we will all eat and drink together.'

'Yes, tea and coffee,' Penaud said, winking at me. 'When I think what you have on the *River Ghost*.'

'Don't bother, Captain Penaud,' I said. 'Musbewi's had the lot.'

'Ah. He was ever a man for the main chance. Well, we can talk about what happened at his camp later. There's plenty of time. For now, I want to enjoy some pleasant company, especially yours, Mademoiselle.'

*

Pieters was coming round. He could feel each of his arms and for a moment he thought it had just been a bad dream. Then he looked at the dressing where an arm had been, and a bitter reality rose up in him again. Someone was standing over him, a white face that was not Schweitzer's. It was much younger.

'I'm Gillespie,' the man said.

'Yeah, I remember now. The young doctor.'

'Well, not quite.'

'Not quite?'

Pieters looked at Gillespie suspiciously as he was helped to sit up.

'I'm a medical student,' Gillespie said, 'I'm not yet qualified.'

'But Schweitzer thought you were okay for me, huh? The great man couldn't soil his hands on a man like me?'

'You know very well he's not like that.'

'Do I? He treats the blacks here like children, I know that much. Acting like a bloody saint.'

'There are far worse ways to treat them. You need to calm down and keep still now. I need to check your dressing.'

'Why did you take my arm off? It was only a goddamn scratch.'

Pieters' head was pounding. It kept time with the rain now thundering down on the hospital roof. He wanted his arm back. He wanted this to be all a dream from which he'd wake up in his hammock on the coast after a good drink.

'It was far more than a scratch,' Gillespie said. 'You had gangrene. Amputating the arm was the only way to save your life. Dr. Schweitzer has already told you that.'

'Yeah, that's what you say. Maybe Schweitzer just wanted it that way. Maybe it was my punishment for offending him, for mocking his rules of so-called decency. Christ, I need a drink. How about some whisky, you could at least give me that after taking my arm.'

'You know Lambaréné is a dry place.'

'You must have some medicinal stuff. Where's Hope? Tell him I want to see him.'

'Mr. Hope doesn't have any liquor either, if that's what you're thinking. Musbewi took all he had, apparently.'

'Musbewi! Hope should have killed that old bastard too, not pay him off.'

'I still need to check your dressing,' Gillespie said. 'If you don't want another infection to set in you'd better let me do my job.'

As Gillespie checked his wound Pieters' head started to clear. By the time he was given something to ease his pain Pieters knew what he was going to do. A plan was forming.

*

My meeting with Penaud was not as difficult as I'd expected it to be. Twenty years earlier there wouldn't have even been a meeting or questions to answer. A white man killing a black man would hardly register. That was a tragedy then, just as it was now. I had hoped to carve out a new start, and maybe even a new life in Gabon, but it seemed broken now.

I went over the details of the *incident,* as Penaud called it. I told him what had happened as precisely and as honestly as I could. Penaud took notes, pausing a few times to shake his head or tut-tut. I was the first to be interviewed. Schweitzer said that Pieters was in no fit state to talk rationally yet.

'Was he ever?' Penaud said. 'That man has caused trouble from the first day he got here, but weren't you once friendly with him, Mr. Hope?'

'Never friendly, but yes, we did drink together from time to time, when I first arrived. He's done some good work on the *River Ghost* for me, and I didn't know him very well then. He was more sober in those days too.'

'Well, his old job is gone for him now. For a man who works with his hands to lose one of them is an endgame, surely?'

'Yes.'

'I think I have enough information from you. Sadly, you are the one who has paid for Pieters' sins, as it were.'

'The man who died paid a much greater price.'

'Quite so.'

'Were you in the war, Penaud?'

'Not on active service. I was stationed here to round up any hostile nationals who might be in the territory.' Penaud lowered his voice. 'The Schweitzers were included, which was rather embarrassing. He's always seemed more French than German to me. I'm glad he came back. It's an amazing thing he's doing here.'

'Indeed. What about Pieters? What will happen to him now?'

'If the man was French we'd probably deport him back to the slum he came from, but my report will probably be filed and forgotten. As for you, it is a clear case of self-defence. Musbewi will try to get compensation of course, and the authorities will probably give it to him. He'll be reminding me about this business every time the *Alemba* goes up there.'

'I hope some of it gets to that man's wife.'

'I wouldn't bet on it.'

After I'd signed it, Penaud folded my statement and put it carefully in an official looking file.

'Is that really all that happens when a man is killed here?

'What would you prefer? To be tried for manslaughter? I am fifty-six years old, Mr. Hope, and have been out here most of my adult life. The locals were still eating each other when I first arrived. Back then the tribes used to clash over the slightest thing. They took any insult very seriously, and life was cheap. It is still cheap. The strange thing was that trouble would subside as quickly as it started, and no one seemed to hold grudges.'

'But that was *their* world. It still is. Do you think things are any better now? And who's to say what is better anyway?'

'Well, they are safer, certainly. We've brought a kind of civilization, I suppose.'

'You sound sceptical yourself, Penaud?'

'Of course I am, but for men like myself it's difficult to change. I was born into a very different time. The slave trade had finished not that long before my time, and you could say Gabon was at the heart of that terrible business. Slaves were its best export.'

Penaud stopped to light up a cigarette, but I turned down the one he offered me.

'Now people come to take other things out of Africa,' Penaud continued. 'You want the timber, the French government wants order, and Schweitzer wants souls, and they are very slippery customers indeed. I do think he's a great man, but his position here is complicated. I'm aware that back home some people think he wants too much. Not everyone thinks that Schweitzer is a saint, you know.'

'But a lot do.'

'So I'm told, but there's a lot of misunderstanding about his role here, maybe even resentment. Amie Moreau feels a bit like that.'

'What do you mean?'

'She represents a new kind of thinking.'

'Which is what?'

'She thinks that Schweitzer wants the people here to be moulded into an image he likes. One that suits *his* philosophy and *his* faith.'

'Is that such a bad thing? And how do you know that anyway?'

'We talked a bit about it at Cape Lopez.'

'What about you, Penaud? What do you think?'

'I think a hospital here was desperately needed. If Schweitzer brings God with him to achieve it, then so be it.'

'Penaud, don't take this the wrong way, but I never realised you were so deep.'

'You get a lot of time to think going up and down the river. You can appreciate that.'

'Yes.'

'I don't have a complicated job here. I just deliver people and goods, and write an occasional report on incidents like yours.'

'You keep calling it an *incident*. A killing is far more than that, isn't it?'

'Yes, but after so many millions killed in the war, one more violent death in an obscure African backwater does not bother me overmuch.'

But it does me, I thought. There was no point in saying anything else to Penaud. He was a man hardened to the life here in a way I never could be. This came to me quite suddenly, and it was a good moment.

'I confiscate a lot of things too,' Penaud said, 'and soon there will be a decent pension waiting for me.'

'The traditional carrot on a stick,' I said.

'Precisely. We are all donkeys, no?'

'So, will you live in Paris?'

'Good God, no. That place is far too busy for me. I'll go back to Bordeaux, where I grew up. It's a fine town.'

'You never married?'

'No, I was never that unfortunate.'

That made me smile. Schweitzer was right. Despite his deep-rooted cynicism, Penaud was decent enough, and good company.

'God, I could use a drink,' I said, 'a proper drink.'

'You really have nothing left on board?'

'Not a drop.'

'Well I have a few bottles in my cabin on the *Alemba*. Emergency supplies, you might say. You can join me later if you want.'

'That's very civilised of you, Penaud.'

Penaud pushed back his thinning hair. It had once been black, but was now streaked with grey, and had a light film of grease on it to hold in place. He smiled back at me, and I noticed his teeth were in remarkably good condition after a lifetime here.

'So, you have met Amie Moreau, eh?' Penaud said. 'She's a warm one.'

'Do you know much about her?'

'I know that much. A few of the officials on the coast tried to get to know her better, if you get my drift. She encouraged it, but then she played them all for fools.'

'A bit of a tease, then?'

'Let's just say she is a young Parisienne for the new age. I might be stranded out here but I still read the Paris papers, even if they are a month out of date.'

Penaud stood up and gave me a mock salute.

'Well, that officially concludes my investigation, Mr. Hope. Or shall it be Adam?'

'If you like. And yours?'

'Ah, I never use it. Penaud is fine.'

'So you don't think there will be any more questions after you file that report?'

'From those higher up, you mean? I shouldn't think so. You haven't annoyed too many people here, have you?'

'You mean too many white people?

'Of course.'

'Not really.'

'Well, there we have it.'

I could hear movement in the next room and then we were five as Amie, Gillespie and Schweitzer joined us.

'Are you finished, Penaud?' Schweitzer asked. 'Is everything in order?'

'Certainly, Doctor, though I will want to talk to Pieters as soon as he's ready. We need to take that man off the Ogowe for good now.'

'Yes. Dinner will be served shortly.'

Before I joined the others for the meal I excused myself by saying I had to get something from the *River Ghost*. I needed to collect my senses after the meeting with Penaud. Julius was waiting for me on deck.

'All okay, boss? I don't think you go white man's jail, not for killing no crazy black man.'

This was the saddest thing anyone had ever said to me. And the fact Julius said it made it even sadder. It told me the hard road that lay ahead if this country was to change in the way people like Amie Moreau wanted, and in truth, the way I wanted.

When I got back to Schweitzer's house food was about to be served. I could smell fresh bread, one of the better things the French had introduced here. I knew from my first stay at Lambaréné that Joseph had become adept at baking it, taking it on himself to train up whatever helpers were in Schweitzer's kitchen.

Now that Gillespie was back at Lambaréné I would sleep on the *River Ghost*, but first I'd join Penaud for a few drinks on board the *Alemba*, which was moored close by.

I sat alongside the Frenchman and Amie sat opposite me. She tried to trap me with her eyes as much as possible. I could feel them on me all the time. Schweitzer began an earnest theological discussion with Gillespie, whilst the rest of us concentrated on the food. I soon realised that the Oxford man shared Schweitzer's religious devotion. Penaud made an occasional wry comment but Amie and I were silent.

'You are very quiet, Mr. Hope,' Schweitzer said, as we followed the food with coffee from the doctor's large silver pot. It came all the way from Alsace, he told us.

'Well, he's got a lot to think about,' Gillespie said, 'after what happened in Musbewi's camp.'

145

'Well, *I'm* thinking more of our drinks later,' Penaud whispered to me in French, which he knew Gillespie didn't understand.

I hoped Schweitzer did not hear it, but Amie certainly did. She let out a little giggle, and I felt her foot probing mine under the table. Schweitzer looked on with that benign expression that rarely left his face.

'Yes, it *is* a lot to think about, Mr. Gillespie,' I finally answered.

I expected a further challenge from Gillespie but he kept his powder dry, for now.

'Do you mind if the men smoke now, Mademoiselle?' Schweitzer said.

'Of course not, Doctor, and this woman will join you.'

We moved into Schweitzer's living-cum-music room, where the air soon turned blue with tobacco smoke.

'Well, Doctor,' Penaud said, 'I think you know what I would like now. I think we all would.' Penaud nodded towards the piano. 'It would be the perfect way to end the evening.'

'As you wish,' Schweitzer said.

He sat at the piano and began to play, a brittle but sweet sound that soon filled the room. When I'd first heard the doctor's music, with a disinterested Jan Pieters, I'd let it waft over me without thinking about it too much. I'd thought it pleasant but not much else. Tonight was different.

Penaud was obviously a lover of Bach. He listened with eyes closed and hands clasped as Schweitzer warmed up. The soothing music linked up with the rain outside to create a restful atmosphere, but there was something much deeper to it than that. After a few minutes Schweitzer seemed to become one with the music he was creating. He became part of its texture, and he pulled us in with him. Even Amie.

We were all lost in our thoughts as much as the music, and for once mine were not disturbing. I was able to lock away the war and the killing upstream for a while, and follow the doctor's progress through each composition.

Schweitzer was on a musical journey, seamlessly moving from one piece to the next, dovetailing them together perfectly, and barely looking at the music spread out on his piano. He obviously knew this music by heart, and was drawing on his many past concert performances. Schweitzer was enjoying himself as much as we were. There was even a touch of the showman about him as he connected with his muse. Listening to him play, I felt at peace. I think we all did.

Schweitzer paused his performance.

'I miss playing the organ,' he said. 'Having the piano here is a blessing indeed, but the organ...'

He let the sentence trail off.

'Won't you play some more, Doctor?' Penaud said.

'Maybe later, but right now I need my pipe, Captain Penaud. Bach always does that to me.'

'You play beautifully,' Amie said.

'Thank you, my dear. Personally, I think I'm a little rusty.'

'How do you manage to do so much?' Amie said.

'So much?'

'Yes, the music, your books, your work here? I'm finding it difficult to do even one thing.'

'Which is what?'

Amie reddened slightly. 'I'm also trying to write a book. A novel actually.'

'Indeed? How interesting. Will it be set in Gabon?'

'Partly. That's why I'm here.'

'I see.'

'Well, you'll have plenty of subject matter,' Penaud said. He tapped me on the shoulder. 'Be careful, Adam, Mademoiselle Moreau might put you in her book. You gave her a great scene the other night.'

This was greeted with silence. Schweitzer lit his pipe and sucked vigorously on it. Gillespie looked at the doctor, and then at me. I expected him to respond, but he too remained quiet. Even so, there was no getting away from a killing.

*

Pieters heard the piano, a fragile but insistent sound coming out of the night. At first he thought it was inside his head, yet another thing to torment him, but his mind was clearing now. The pain from the amputation saw to that. It was a throbbing, pulsating pain that broke through the fug of his medication to announce its presence and tell him that his arm was gone. You're a cripple, it said, what good will *you* be here? What good will you be anywhere?

Pieters looked around the room. It was almost bare, but there were a few surgical tools on a table in the corner. A knife caught his eye. It was a short blade that he knew would be sharp.

Pieters took three attempts to get up. Pain from his phantom arm seared into his shoulder. He felt as if it was being taken off again, ripped off by a river croc that had clamped its jaws on it and taken him for a spin. Rolling him over and over in that deadly way they had of killing their prey.

Pieters gritted his teeth as he steadied himself on the edge of the bed. It was hard to keep his balance, because his body did not feel right. It was out of kilter, weight was missing from one side, but he made it to the table and picked up the knife.

Holding the knife in his hand, he felt the cold touch of the blade as he pressed it against his forehead. It calmed him, and strengthened his resolve. Self-pity began to fuel his rage as all kinds of things raced through his mind. They had taken off his arm for no good reason. Schweitzer had lied about the infection. That doctor-cum-holy man had wanted to be judge and jury and had found him guilty.

Schweitzer didn't fool Pieters. That German made out he was a saviour of the blacks, but he was no different to any other colonial out here. He was just another man on the make, but he had more angles than most chancers. Schweitzer served himself, not his fucking God, the pompous bastard. Yes, it was all becoming clear to him now. With one arm he'd have no choice but to go home, and that was what they wanted, because that way he'd be out of their hair for good.

Pieters listened carefully by the door. He could hear voices, but they were faint and some distance away. They barely carried over the sound of the rain as it hammered down, playing crazy rhythms on the metal roof. Another intense burst of pain surged through him. It caused him to gasp, and steady himself against the door. No, it's not my arm, he thought, my arm isn't there any more.

Pieters stepped outside, letting the rain strike his face. He looked up at the black sky for it to cool him. He could hear the piano clearly now. It must be the doctor playing. This meant they would all be in the living room. He edged along the veranda, putting the knife in his belt. It was necessary, for he needed to hold onto things with his remaining arm.

The music stopped and there was sound of a door opening. He recognised Hope's voice, and flattened himself against the wall as Hope walked down the steps of the house with that French captain. They were trying to shelter under an umbrella.

Scrunching up his eyes against the rain, Pieters watched them walk down to the river to board the *Alemba*. Faint yellow deck lights allowed it to emerge out of the gloom, its twin paddle wheels looming over the smaller *River Ghost*. Pieters grasped the knife again and gritted his teeth against the pain.

*

Penaud made a pretence of holding his umbrella over both of us, but he was much shorter than me and I was still soaked by the time we got down to the riverbank. My feet were also wet, for when it rained like this the ground became saturated very quickly. Water sprang from its surface in countless small rivulets, one of which penetrated my shoes with ease.

'Come aboard, Captain,' Penaud said, sweeping me up the gangplank with a flourish. 'You'll find the *Alemba* quite spacious compared to that tub of yours.'

Penaud was right. He showed me into what he laughingly called the stateroom, but it was far bigger than my cabin on the *Ghost*. One of his men appeared with a towel, which the

Frenchman threw at me. As I dried my head and face he opened up a liquor cabinet, a squat wooden affair with ornate carvings on it. I was impressed when I saw the array of drinks it held.

'I thought you said you only had a few bottles,' I said. 'It's more like a bar, I'm glad to say.'

'This was originally a spice box,' Penaud said, 'I confiscated it from an Arab smuggler on the coast. Whisky? I'm sure that will be your drink of choice.'

'It is.'

He poured me a liberal drink, almost three fingers of Black and White whisky, which I hadn't seen since the war.

'Where the hell did you get that?' I said.

'Oh, I confiscated this too. Lots of contraband comes my way, Adam. People here pay for their sins in a variety of ways, and as an official of the French government, it's my duty to receive.'

'Yes, I bet.'

'My pension will not be over generous, so one must find ways to supplement it.'

Penaud poured himself a Pernod.

'This is *my* drink of choice,' he said.

I sat down on one of the two comfortable armchairs Penaud had in his spacious cabin.

'So, it's been an interesting day,' Penaud said, 'or rather a few days.'

'I'd use other words to describe it.'

'Quite. Pieters loses an arm, Musbewi a tribesman, and you almost get killed. Oh, and Amie Moreau is writing a book. I've never been much of a reader myself. Are you?'

'Not for a long time, but yes, in my youth, and in the war, when I could get something worth reading.'

'Something tells me that she won't be very kind to Gabon — the French here, anyway.'

I raised my glass. 'I'll drink to that.'

'Do I detect the whiff of support for her views?'

'More like a stench, I'd say.'

'Ah, two young rebel minds in unison. Bodies too, perhaps?'

Penaud smiled when I didn't answer. He moved his drink around in his glass, a slow swirl of cloudy liquid that he was obviously savouring before drinking. My large glass of Black and White was already much diminished, prompting Penaud to top it up.

'You are a complicated soul, aren't you?' Penaud said.

'Not particularly.'

'Oh I think so. Sometimes I think I'm the only European out here who isn't running away from something. For you it's the war, and who could blame you for that, but maybe also from other things?'

'Is this the policeman asking?'

'No, just one riverboat captain to another.'

'There's nothing unique about me, Penaud. I had an early relationship that failed, and then came the war. That's hardly rare, is it?'

'Not at all, but I still think everyone who comes to Africa is a little lost, or mad — or both.'

Penaud sipped his Pernod, but much slower than I attacked my whisky. The drink was hitting me now, moving around my system on its usual fiery course. Another large one and I would almost be drunk, but that was fine by me.

'You are quite different to any other white man I know who works the Ogowe,' Penaud said. 'Of course, you are the only Englishman here — sorry, Welshman. I keep forgetting that. Is there any real difference?'

'Some might say so. Quite virulently.'

'Ah. A bit like our Basques down south then, or those pesky Bretons. Another drink?'

I held out my glass, more eagerly than I intended.

'This had better be my last,' I said. 'Make it a small one.'

Penaud finished his own drink with a slight smack of his lips.

'Ah, Pernod. It's been the ruin of many a good Frenchman, especially out here. You'd think we'd have more sense, wouldn't you? Alcohol and heat are never a good match.'

'No, they're not.'

'Yet we do it all the same. The locals have long since discovered drink too, and that makes good business for you.'

'I'd say they were more introduced to it. Schweitzer doesn't approve.'

'Of course not. Why would he? He probably sees it as one more thing to enslave the people here, but I wouldn't let it trouble you. Traders had been plying the people here with drink for decades before you arrived on the river.'

'So I've been told.'

'Do you like the man?'

'Schweitzer? I certainly respect him. He is quite remarkable.'

'Yes, I suppose you could say he's that.'

'You sound sceptical, Penaud.'

'Well, I'm a lot older than you and I've been here a long time. This colony has been paved with good intentions, but often they are a mask for avarice and power, so the results have been mixed, to put it mildly.'

'Surely bringing modern medicine here is vital? I've seen how it helps.'

'Of course it is, but people here survived before us. In the past they were in more danger from slavery than disease.'

'Yes, but slavery has been eradicated.'

'There are many kinds of slavery, my friend.'

'So why not at least concentrate on disease? Schweitzer has made good progress with that, hasn't he?'

'Indeed, and it's amazing the way he's re-building Lambaréné. I didn't expect him to return.'

'So why the reticence?'

'Because in his own way Schweitzer is an empire builder, and I suppose such men unnerve me somewhat. They bring out my cynicism. Schweitzer brings God with him as well. Oh, I know his intentions are good, and that he's not after the usual rewards, but it *is* making him famous, and I don't think he's averse to that. I'm told people are fascinated by what he's doing here, especially the English. You seem to need heroes more than the French.'

'You're doing the English thing again, Penaud.'

There was a knock on the cabin door and the deckhand on watch escorted Amie in.

'Good God,' I said, 'what are *you* doing here, in this weather?'

Amie stood in the doorway, soaked to the skin like I had been. Penaud raised an appreciative glass as he took in the sight. He saw a young woman whose figure was clearly outlined, for her wet dress had become diaphanous. I was surprised he didn't utter *ooh la la*.

'Couldn't you at least have found an umbrella?' I said. 'Penaud, can you get another towel please?'

'With pleasure.'

He left us for a moment, but long enough for Amie to push herself against me, playing her lips against my cheek.

'I just wanted to be with you tonight,' Amie said. 'Why should I be excluded? Hmm, I wonder if Penaud has any more of that?' She nodded towards the empty Pernod bottle. 'A rich man's absinthe,' she muttered, 'but it's not quite as lethal, I'm glad to say.'

'Didn't they ban absinthe?'

'Yes, in the war. It was rotting minds, they said.'

'Whilst millions were being slaughtered? How ironic.'

*

Pieters made slow progress along the muddy walkway. It was hard to see as the rain unloaded on him, and even harder to get his balance. He lurched to the left as he walked. It was as if his body was trying to compensate for its loss. He almost foundered a few times, like a steamboat that had lost its rudder, but he kept going. Hate kept him going.

He kept to the shadows as much as he could. His progress was slow, but his determination made sure it was steady. He was near the *Alemba* now, standing against a low fence that ran close to the river.

Sticking the knife in his belt he turned his face upwards to the night sky for it to be cooled once more. He felt like a man worshipping the night and the rain, rather than the sun. Ahead, deck lights faintly lit up the *Alemba*. They made a yellow glimmer that flickered dimly through the haze that the rain created.

The Frenchwoman almost caught him. Her heard a noise behind him and turned to see her stumbling her way towards the river. He pushed himself further into the shadows, holding onto the stunted remains of a tree with his one hand. A lot of thoughts passed through his mind as that tart from Paris went past, but he would keep to his plan.

She called out as she reached the gangway of the *Alemba*, and a crewman came down to help her aboard. Pieters' feet were sinking into the soft earth, and he could hear lots of movement in the undergrowth. Slithering and rustling was all around him, plus a few muffled snorts. Night creatures were coming alive as the rain eased, and he identified with them. He was one himself.

As Moreau disappeared below deck, Pieters cautiously made his way to the river's edge. The deck hand was back at his station, but he was smoking on the starboard side of the boat and watching the river. That was where danger usually came from, but tonight it would be different. His phantom arm still taunted him, and his exertions had caused his dressing to become unstable. A bandage had started to unravel, and with just one hand there was not much he could do about it. It would have to trail along in the dirt if need be.

Pieters could hear the faint sounds of conversation on the *Alemba*, Penaud's voice mainly. That posturing Frenchman was a clown, and was not worth bothering about. It was Hope that dominated his thoughts. The bastard was in there now, warm, dry, and drinking whisky.

Pieters waited in the shadows of the port side of the *Alemba* for a long time. He almost fainted a few times, as he felt his blood seeping out through his bandages, but his resolve righted him each time. For some crazy reason his past flashed through his mind in countless images.

For the first time in years Pieters saw his father again, the old man in all his rotten glory. He had managed to blot him out since he'd arrived at Cape Lopez nine years ago. He'd always planned to go back and kill the old bastard one day, until his sister who kept in touch told him that he had died. He celebrated that by drinking two bottles of rum.

As he crouched in the darkness thirty years dripped away from Pieters. He saw again that tiny box room his mother had optimistically called a bedroom. He shared it with his sister until he was ten.

Hell started when Pieters was seven, and Saturday nights were the worst. That was his father's only drinking night, when there was just enough money for him to come home sodden with absinthe and cheap beer. Pieters could hear the old man's heavy tread on the bare staircase, desperately hoping that his father would walk past the door to the family bedroom, but he rarely did.

At that age he wasn't really sure what his father was doing to him. His sister Marie would bury herself in bedclothes and press her hands over her ears.

'Pray to God that papa doesn't come tonight,' Marie would tell him. Pieters did pray, but God did not listen. He must have listened to Marie, though, for their father never touched her.

Nor did God hear him when he prayed for his mother to get better. She died when Pieters was six, and he never trusted God again, or believed in Him.

His father made cheap furniture for the back street locals, and they lived over the space he rented for a workshop. It gave the Pieters family a kind of living. Eckerd Pieters was respected in the area, even liked by some, which made him hate his father even more. He hated to way the old man sucked up to people, greeting customers with that stupid attempt at a posh accent. He hated the way he kept that ornate old family bible on the workshop table, so that people who came into the shop could see what an upright man he was. He hated his father full stop.

Pieters got away when he was twelve. He learned to live off scraps and his wits and they had eventually got him to Africa. Now he was alone, one-armed and hurting bad in the mud of an African jungle.

In his fevered mind the image of his father was blending into one of Hope, another upright fucking man. Schweitzer too. They were just as false as his father had been, just from different backgrounds. Richer backgrounds. And the rich knew how to do these things so much better.

The weather changed quickly, as was the Gabon way. Within minutes a clear sky crammed with stars appeared overhead. The jungle was waking up after the rain. It was alive with the countless shrieks of animals going about their business, the business of kill or be killed. How life should be, Pieters thought.

He heard noise and movement on the deck of the *Alemba*. All pain left him as he heard Hope's voice. He was coming down the gangplank and that bitch was almost entwined with him. Pieters' anger went up a notch.

He took the knife from his belt, but thought again when he saw a heavy, gnarled stick that had been discarded on the riverbank. With just one arm it would be easier to use than the knife. It would make a good club.

*

Penaud re-appeared with the towel. It was none too clean but Amie didn't mind. She rubbed vigorously at her hair, and didn't mind re-arranging that either. She was unlike any woman I'd ever met before.

'I'm afraid there is no more Pernod,' Penaud said.

'That's a pity.'

'Indeed it is, but I have a bottle of halfway decent Chablis. I've been keeping it for a special occasion.'

Something bumped against the hull of the *Alemba*, causing the glasses on Penaud's makeshift bar to tremble.

'What's that?' Amie said, holding onto my arm.

'A hippo maybe, or a stray log. Lots of things go bump in the night on the river here.'

Outside, the rain began to ease. The freshness it had brought disappeared with it, and the night began to turn sultry. Sultry was what the jungle did best. I felt my wet shirt starting to steam and stick to me, and I didn't want to drink any more. In fact I didn't even want to be here any more. I wanted to go back to the *River Ghost*, but not alone.

I noticed how slim Amie was, with barely a waist, and legs that were almost as thin as they were long. In the sodden dress that was determined to stick to her she looked very vulnerable, but I knew she was nothing of the sort. Penaud poured her a large glass of Chablis.

'I'm afraid it's a little warm,' Penaud said.

'No matter. It goes with the territory.'

'And you, Adam, some wine?'

'Wine on top of whisky? No thanks.'

We were quiet for a while. The rain had now stopped completely. All we heard was the creaking of the boat, and the chink of a few things on deck as they caught the river breeze. Penaud looked on like a benign priest. He was well into his cups now and he started to nod. His head sank down onto his chest, but he still held his glass firmly, like all good drinkers did.

'Ah,' Amie said, 'the Pernod has finally got to him. I was hoping it would.'

'Why?'

Amie leant over to kiss me, pulling me to her by grasping my shirt.

'Were you born naïve, Adam Hope, or have you worked on it all your life? Come on, let's go.'

'It's a bit rude to just get up and and leave.'

'God, the English and manners. It's a wonder you don't all suffocate. Penaud won't mind at all, in fact he'd probably be disappointed if we didn't disappear.'

We quietly made our way up to the deck, but did not escape the watchful eye of the man stationed there. He saluted me and grinned. It was a case of down one gangplank and up the other, as the *Ghost* was moored just feet away.

'Look,' said Amie, when we got on board, 'the stars are coming out. How bright they are.'

'Yes, they always are after a storm.'

Amie clung onto me as I guided her to the hatchway that led below. I could not see him, but I knew Julius would be watching us from somewhere in the darkness. He would be seeing his captain in a new light.

Maybe my life was finally about to turn, I thought, and I'd have a new road to travel. I felt good but nervous as I kissed Amie on the back of her neck. She was right, the stars really were bright tonight. A thousand pins of white light seemed to fall down on the far edges of the forest.

I sensed a blur to my right. There was movement, and as I turned, something hit me on the side of my head. I was knocked backwards and lurched towards the edge of the boat. I tried to right myself but was pushed over the side by an unseen hand. It shoved me hard in the back and I hit the black water in seconds, and went down.

The water was surprisingly cold, and it hit me even harder than the blow to my head. I managed to come back up to break the surface, kicking hard with my feet, but I felt my shoes being sucked off by the current as I went down again. I was being carried rapidly down stream, too rapidly to resist, and knew I had to stay on the surface if I were ever to stand on dry land again. I'd been a strong swimmer in my late school years, but I hadn't so much as swum a stroke since before the war.

I could not see clearly. Maybe it was the blow to my head, maybe it was the water, the water I was drowning in. As the current tossed me around, despite the blackness all around me, a white sheen seemed to gather above me. I thought this must be the massed stars in the sky, but wasn't sure if they were inside my head or not. The river was sucking at every part of me, and if I went down again I would not resurface. Three was the limit for anyone.

I heard faint shouting in the darkness behind me, but I didn't dare turn my head. I struck out as hard as I could, my lungs screaming at me to stop, and I found a friendlier channel in the river, the current no longer trying to pull me down. Something large loomed up out of the water ahead of me. If it was a hippo that was the end for me.

When I was about to collide with it I stuck out a hand, more in resignation than defence. It was not a hippo. It was a tree half submerged in the river, and the collision knocked the breath from my chest. Even so it was my salvation, and I clutched a branch which had been snarled up on all sorts of other growth to form a barrier. I heaved myself far enough out of the water to grasp the branch with both hands, despite the river's best attempts to wash me away.

I hung on for dear life, barely conscious for a few seconds, until I got some breath back. This time I did look back towards the two riverboats. I was at least a few hundred yards downstream and could see movement along the bank, and lights. Men were carrying lanterns as they scoured the banking. They were looking for me, but no one would be expecting to find me, dead or alive.

I had to get out of the water, for I knew that soon my grip would weaken and I'd be on my way down to the mud. My head was troubling me more now that I had stopped trying to swim. There was a pounding there, as if I was being repeatedly punched. As the lights grew closer I tried to shout, but nothing would come out.

Something large came close by me, and then was gone. I tried to think if crocodiles were present in this part of the river, but I couldn't focus. I could only try to hang on.

The lanterns were as close as they were ever going to get now, so I sucked as much air as I could into my lungs and bellowed. Nothing like a bellow came out, but it was enough for someone on the shore to hear. I could hear shouting, as many voices started to cry out in Galoan. I thought I heard a splash. Something was coming towards me. It must be a croc if it was coming from the banking. No matter, for I felt my hold on the branch was weakening anyway.

Something was holding me. It was the last thing I could remember. I was about to be taken in a death roll by a crocodile. At least it would be quick.

*

Julius ran along the riverbank, followed by Osobu and a few other crewmen. His keen eyes tried to probe the darkness. The river was full to overflowing, and it gleamed silver now that the stars were out. He knew in his heart of hearts there was not much hope for the captain. Soon the sandy banking would turn back into a thick mass of tree roots and undergrowth that would make it impossible for him to continue. He was about to give up when he thought he heard something.

Julius stood still, straining his ears against the rushing of the river, and letting the others catch up with him. He heard it again, coming from the water, from a fallen tree that had stuck fast there. A voice.

'Shut up all of you,' Julius said.

Osobu almost collided with Julius as he'd come to a sudden dead stop.

'There it is again,' Julius said, 'that's the boss shouting.' He pointed a hand towards Hope's saviour tree.

Osobu shrugged. 'I can't hear anything.'

Julius grabbed his arm. 'Yes you can. We all can.'

Osobu shrugged his arm off. 'Would he try to save you? Would any of *them* try to save one of us?'

Julius did not answer. He held up his lantern and could see there was either a body snagged on a branch, or someone holding onto it.

'There. He's there.'

Julius did not hesitate. He handed the lantern to Osobu, kicked off his sandals and dived into the water. He cut through the water with a flurry of powerful strokes and soon reached Hope. Julius wedged himself against the tree as he reached out for his captain.

'Boss! I've got you.'

Julius held Hope up, fighting hard against the down flow of the water. The boss was barely conscious now, but he was holding on tight. They were both holding on tight.

It was five minutes before a dugout got to them, but it seemed like a lifetime to Julius. His body was almost numb as strong arms took Hope from him and hauled the captain aboard. Then Osobu reached out a hand to pull Julius up. They locked eyes. Julius knew Osobu thought him a fool, but he made his own choices. Osobu was wrong, the captain had saved him when the log raft had broken free, and Julius had not forgotten that. Now a debt had been repaid.

When they got to the bank Gillespie was waiting, and so was a frantic Amie.

'Make room there,' Gillespie shouted, as Amie ran to Hope's side.

'Adam? Are you okay?'

She held onto Hope but he was barely aware of it.

Gillespie gently moved her away and shook Hope a few times to bring him around.

'He's all right, I think,' Gillespie said, 'but he has swallowed a lot of river water, and God knows what's in that. You men carry him back to the hospital. The doctor is waiting.'

Penaud appeared at the scene, a little unsteady on his feet.

'I hope Pieters has been well secured, Captain?' Gillespie asked.

'Yes. It wasn't hard. He'd lost so much blood that he could barely stand. I think the last of his strength was used up in the attack.'

'Why would Pieters want to kill the man who saved his life?' Amie said. 'Why, for God's sake? He just appeared out of the darkness.'

'Killers usually do,' Penaud murmured. 'Maybe in his warped mind he blames Adam for the loss of his arm. Pieters is not the type of man to take responsibility for anything. It's a pity he didn't go overboard himself, for I doubt that anyone would try to save *that* man.'

Schweitzer was waiting when the small crowd of men and one woman arrived at the hospital.

'Where is Pieters?' Schweitzer said.

'I've kept him on the *Alemba,* Doctor,' Penaud said.

'Well, go get him, man. He will need treatment too.'

Gillespie and Julius supported Hope up the steps to the hospital, and Amie kept close by them. Schweitzer noted the fear and concern on her face. He was disturbed by this further development of violence. First the tragic business upriver, and now an attempted murder at Lambaréné. He had not known anything like this before, and it was the same two men that were involved. It was a poor example to show the people here.

Schweitzer gave Adam Hope a thorough examination. The man was bruised all over his body, but they were superficial injuries. He had taken a heavy blow to the head, which would have to be monitored, but the main danger would be if he contracted a disease from the river water, for the Ogowe carried all sorts of unacceptable material. Hope could be at risk from typhoid, hepatitis, and many other dangerous things, but he was young and strong. Surviving that long in the swollen river had proved that.

'No, don't try to speak, Adam,' Schweitzer said as Hope showed signs of stirring. 'I don't think the blow to your head has caused any serious problems, but you've been very lucky, very lucky indeed. I'll give you something to help you sleep now. Rest is what you need.'

Hope still tried to sit up, but Schweitzer's hand was firm and strong, so he settled him back on the bed until the drug did its work. They were bringing Pieters in to another room. The man was in a pitiful state, delirious and muttering incoherently.

'Can you remove what's left of his bandages, please?' Schweitzer said to Gillespie, 'and then we'll see what can be done for this man.'

Penaud stayed on Schweitzer's veranda with Amie. He lit up a cigar and exhaled a long line of smoke into the night as Amie remained standing, lost in thought.

'Well, Mr. Hope has had rather a dramatic few days, hasn't he?'

Amie did not answer. She was gazing at the shadowy wall of the jungle, and the river that cut through it, the one that had almost taken the man she wanted.

'I thought I'd lost him,' she muttered, after a silence long enough for Penaud to smoke his cigar half way down.

'Hope is a survivor. He was in the war from start to finish, you know. All the French officers I knew seemed to last only a matter of weeks.'

'Has he told you much about himself?'

'Not really, apart from he doesn't like being taken for an Englishman.'

'Yes, I know that. He hasn't been married though, has he?'

'No, Mademoiselle.' Penaud smiled and tapped Amie on the shoulder. 'Not yet.'

Schweitzer joined them for a moment.

'How is he, Doctor?' Amie said.

'There's been no real damage done. I'll need to carefully monitor him, though, in case he's picked up anything from the river water.'

'Can I see him?'

'Best let him sleep now. In the morning would be better. Joseph will serve coffee for you in the living room. I must help Gillespie attend to Pieters, but then I'll join you.'

'I hope Pieters will do us a favour,' Penaud muttered, once Schweitzer was out of hearing range.

'What do you mean?'

'Die, of course. Hope's man wanted to throw the Belgian in the river. He would have done it, too, if I hadn't stopped him.'

'Why did you?'

Penaud shrugged. 'It would mean more paperwork.'

'What will happen to Pieters, if he does live?'

'Oh, after attempted murder, and what happened at Musbewi's camp, they'll probably send him across the pond to Devil's Island. You know about that place?'

'A little.'

'A little is all you want to know. Believe me, if Pieters had a choice, he'd prefer to die here, tonight.'

They left the veranda as the next wave of rain began. Joseph was already waiting for them in the living room with his tray.

'Ah, coffee,' Penaud said, 'there's nothing like the smell of it, particularly after a night like this. To me it smacks of comfort, and safety, although of course it often lies. Come, sit down, Amie — may I call you Amie?'

'Of course.'

'I will serve you coffee from this formidable old pot Schweitzer has. It's built like a tank, and isn't it sweet that he has such fine crockery? Sometimes when I'm here I think I'm in a drawing room back home.'

'Where's that?'

'Bordeaux, but I haven't been back for many years. The *Alemba* is really my home now. I have a place down on the coast, but that's just a convenience. I share it with a few other French colonials, a boring lot they are too.'

'This is good coffee,' Amie said.

'Yes, courtesy of Adam Hope. God knows how he manages to get hold of the stuff, but I'm sure the good doctor is grateful.'

'Do you approve of Adam's activities here?'

'I'm non-committal. I learned not to judge a man too quickly a long time ago. One thing I can tell you is that he's not like any other trader here. Oh, he looks to make a good profit, but he's not really a man of business.'

'What is he then?'

'A man running away.'

'From the war?'

'Yes, obviously that, but he's troubled by many things, I think. A bit of a lost soul, you might say. I doubt that Gabon will prove much of a refuge for him now, though, not after the last few days. That young man will have to search inside himself for answers. Life never lets you off the hook that easily. He has empathy for the people here, too, and that also complicates things.'

'I'd say it was admirable.'

'Maybe so, but the *ancien régime* here don't think like that. New ideas will take a long time to work their way out here, if they ever do. It's okay for missionaries to have such notions, but for a white trader to have those views — well, it's unheard of.'

'Yes, I learned that in Cape Lopez.'

'It's almost as bad as having a conscience.'

'You are a cynical old rogue, Monsieur Penaud.'

Penaud raised his coffee cup in a mock salute.

'*Touché*, Amie.'

'Are you *really*, though, Penaud, or is it just an act? It's hard to be sure with a man like you.'

'I'll take that as a compliment, my dear. What about you? Why are *you* really here? Are you yet another refugee, a refugee from yourself, maybe?'

Amie sipped her coffee and looked beyond Penaud to the window. She saw the night outside growing wild again, and the rain beating down on the roof seemed also to beat inside her head. She had thought Adam was dead when they dragged him from the river. She felt like crying, which was very unusual for her.

'Ah, I've upset you,' Penaud said. 'I'm sorry.'

'It's not you, Penaud; I find you quite a comfort, actually. It's just what has happened. I came here looking for action, adventure I suppose, like a stupid schoolgirl.'

'And now it doesn't seem so grand, eh?'

'No.'

'But you have good subject matter for your book.'

'If I ever write it.'

'But you have found love here, is that not the case?'

Penaud fumbled in his pockets, not expecting Amie to answer.

'Damn, I thought I had another cigar,' he said. 'Well, I'm not walking down to the *Alemba* in this weather to get one.'

'Maybe the doctor can oblige?'

'I doubt it. Schweitzer is a pipe man.'

'Do I hear my name being mentioned?' Schweitzer said, as he entered the room.

'Penaud is just bemoaning his lack of cigars,' Amie said.

'Ah, I sympathise, Penaud. A man should never be without tobacco. I have a number of pipes here. You are welcome to try one.'

'No thank you, Doctor. I did once, but they are not for me. How is Pieters?'

'We've replaced his dressing and bandages but he's running a fever, and he's in shock, a bit like some of the poor soldiers I saw in the war. The ones that were sent back from the trenches. I think his mind has been greatly affected by all that has happened.'

'Well, if he lives his freedom will also be affected.'

'If Mr. Hope presses charges. Isn't that how the law works?'

'Surely he will? He almost died.'

'I'm not so sure. Hope is an unusual young man. And you, Amie, have you recovered from this ordeal?'

'Yes, I think so. Thank you, Doctor.'

'Talking about charges,' Penaud said, 'if Julius hadn't intervened, Pieters might have attacked Amie too — in fact I'm sure he would. That man needs putting away for good.'

Schweitzer lit up his pipe, causing Penaud's craving to kick in even more.

'It's been a tragic few days,' Schweitzer said. 'Sometimes I think I'm building a haven here, a place where the kinder aspects of humanity can be nurtured. Then another reality sets in, and I realise the world is a slaughterhouse and always has been. It distresses me so.'

There was an awkward silence and Amie wasn't sure if the doctor was talking to them or himself. She gave Penaud a quizzical look, as Schweitzer's eyes seemed to be almost closed as he spoke. He drew heavily on his pipe, and if a man could be in raptures and also wracked by sadness at the same time, Schweitzer was that man.

A new storm was brewing, and a strong wind now supported the rain. Schweitzer's house was shaking on its iron piles and something crashed down outside, a metallic series of sounds that came out of the night like a fusillade of rifle shots.

'That's probably the roof of one of the outhouses gone' Schweitzer said. 'Something falls prey to a storm every year at Lambaréné, but the hospital will be secure. It's the strongest building here, I've made sure of that.'

'We are not in the hospital,' Penaud muttered.

Gillespie joined them. He looked gaunt and tired, and much older than the student he was.

'I'm afraid the coffee is all gone,' Schweitzer said.

'No matter,' Gillespie said. 'Dr. Schweitzer says you are staying with us tonight, Miss Moreau, so I have prepared my room for you, as best I can.'

'There was no need for that,' Amie, 'I'm sure there is room for me on the *Alemba*.'

'Yes, but you don't want to go out again on a night like this.'

'Okay, thank you, Mr. Gillespie. Do you mind if I retire now, Doctor? I'm very tired.'

'Of course, Mademoiselle. Joseph will show you the way.'

On cue, Joseph appeared in the doorway. He led the way to Gillespie's room by lamplight. It was small and austere, as she had known it would be. Joseph put the small lantern down on a table.

'Tell me, Joseph,' Amie said, 'did Mr. Hope sleep here when he first stayed with you?'

'Yes, missy.'

'Thank you. Good night.'

Joseph shut the door quietly, and for the first time in what seemed an age Amie was alone. She sat down on the edge of the bed and this time she did cry. Fear, relief and hope became one emotion, and tears were the only things she had to deal with it at this moment. She composed herself within minutes, and quietly left the room.

In all the excitement Amie had forgotten to thank Julius for saving Adam. Julius had just slipped away after he brought Adam back to the shore. The man needed to be thanked.

Amie was glad of the umbrella that was propped up against the wall. She did not want another soaking, but she almost slipped on the sodden and treacherous ground. She made her way down to the *River Ghost* as carefully as she could. No one was around apart from a man standing on the deck of Adam's steamboat. It was Julius. He hurried down to help here safely on board.

'Why are you here, miss?' Julius said. 'It's dangerous for you to be out alone in the dark.'

'Oh, I don't think Mr. Pieters will trouble anyone again.'

'There are lots of things here to trouble you at night,' Julius said.

Amie stretched out her hand and touched Julius on the shoulder. She could just about reach it.

'I had to thank you, Julius. I should have done so earlier but—'

'Thanks are not necessary, miss.'

Amie stared at Julius, puzzled at first.

'There's something different about you,' Amie said. 'It's the way you are talking, it's different.'

'You mean it's not pidgin French filled with nonsense words?'

'No, it's not. Look, can we go inside, please, before I too float down the river?'

'Of course.'

Julius led the way to Hope's cabin, which was warm and dry. Amie took the chair she was offered, smoothing out her wet dress over her long legs. She stared at Julius.

'You're not what you seem, are you?' Amie said.

Julius stood impassively before her, shrugging his shoulders slightly.

'Are you playing a role, a role for the white man? I've seen you in that ridiculous hat and jacket you wear, like a black man eager to please. You've had an education, haven't you?'

'Yes.'

Without being asked Julius sat down in the chair opposite Amie. It was an action that might have got him shot in the company of some whites on the coast.

'Yes, I have been educated. My father made sure of that, as much as he could.'

'Then why this?' Amie raised her hands in question.

'When I came down to the coast I realised that an educated black man might be seen as a threat to the whites. I have had to tread carefully to get where I am.'

'Hmm.'

'Have you heard of André Raponda Walker?'

'No. Who is he?'

'He's a great man, and my inspiration. He had a white father and became a priest here, about twenty years ago. He was the first of our people to do that.'

'That's remarkable.'

'Yes, but you still haven't heard of him, have you? I think you should broaden your research here, Miss Amie.'

'Yes, maybe I should.'

'I met Walker once, when I first travelled down the Ogowe. Well, I sought him out really, because one of our French teachers spoke of him. He welcomed me, and we talked for a long time. He told me of how our country might be some day, if we ever get the chance. He speaks a lot of the languages of the people here — I only speak two.'

'And French. You speak that very well, by the way.'

'Thank you.'

Amie was taken aback by the change in Julius. As he talked, his face became animated, it was alive with ideas and the need to get them across. She wondered if she was the first white person he had revealed himself to, and if so, why had he picked her. Julius was no longer the eager-to-please backup man of Adam Hope in the clown-like naval costume.

Amie realised they were talking as equals, and she felt inspired by this, like she'd been when she'd first entered the jazz cellars of Paris. She could imagine the shock, if not horror, on her mother's face if she could witness this scene.

'Walker plans to study our heritage, when he has the time,' Julius said. 'He says that is the way forward for us, to know our true past, and not the one the French want us to have.'

'Isn't your history handed down orally here?' Amie said, 'from generation to generation?'

'Yes, but Walker wants to change that, and he has the learning to do it.'

'And you too?

'Walker is much more learned than I am, but I would like to help one day.'

'So why are you here? Working for Hope on this barge?'

'It might not seem much to you, but it is a fine job for someone like me. The boss pays well, usually, and I can help my family. Maybe one day have a wife.'

Amie touched Julius lightly on his knee, stretching across a hand that suddenly seemed very white to her.

'I did not mean to belittle you in any way, Julius,' she said. 'I just don't think it's necessary to keep your true self a secret.'

'I can assure you it is, miss, and secret from the rest of the crew as much as Captain Hope. It would mark me out as being different, and that is dangerous. It makes you a target, and already some of the men are suspicious of me. One asked me if I could read the other day. He'd seen me looking at a French newspaper.'

'I think I understand, but you have taken a chance telling me.'

'Yes, maybe because of what had happened tonight. I sense that you are... I don't know the word in French...'

'*Sympathique*?'

'Yes, *sympathique*.'

'I'm glad that you think I am. I'd better get back now, to Adam.'

Julius smiled. 'He is your man now?'

'Yes.'

'I'll see you safely back to the doctor's house.'

'There's no need.'

'Yes, there is.'

The rain had abated but Julius still held the umbrella high above her, like the servant he purported to be. On the steps of Schweitzer's house Amie hesitated before she went inside.

'Julius, what do you think of the doctor?' she said quietly.

Julius thought for a while. 'I think he is necessary for our country at this time.'

'Goodnight, Julius, and thank you again.'

'Goodnight, miss.'

As Julius disappeared into the night Amie changed her mind and crossed over to the hospital, just about keeping her footing on the treacherous walkway. The hospital doorway was lit by faint lamplight, but it was enough to guide her way.

Inside, a gently snoring attendant was sleeping on a hard wooden chair by the front door. Amie glided past him. Maybe it was luck, maybe it was fate, but the first door she tried led her to Adam. Fighting down the instinct to hug him, she sat down on the chair by the bed, moving it as close to him as she could.

Adam was sleeping deeply, so she touched him as lightly as possible on the side of his face, pushing his hair away from it. Then she moved her hand all over it, like a blind person trying to gauge someone's appearance. It did not disturb Hope's deep sleep.

Practically nothing had happened between them yet, but Amie knew the bond was now unbreakable, on her part at least. She stared at him for some time. Penaud was right, this was the last thing she'd expected in Gabon, and that made it even sweeter.

Amie heard moaning from the adjacent room. She guessed that Pieters must be in there, but she did not want to look on that man. She might be tempted to do more than that, otherwise. The image of Adam being struck and then falling into the river would be a vivid one forever. Julius had appeared out of the darkness, as suddenly as Pieters, and he had knocked the Belgian down with a heavy blow of his fist. He was about to grind his face with a heel, too, but Amie stopped him, screaming at him to save Adam, if he could. Julius had done just that, and was a hero to her now, even more so after revealing his true self.

With this comforting thought Amie rested her head on the side of the bed. She was sleeping as soundly as Hope within minutes, but would be up and gone before Adam woke up.

*

Schweitzer sat up late this night. Penaud had brought him various correspondences and some much-needed funds from

Paris, but pride of place was another long letter from his wife. He finally had time to read it in peace.

Schweitzer lit his first pipe of the evening and settled back in his armchair, giving thanks as he did so for the new pack of tobacco he had received. He would be lost without it. Helene had also included a new photograph of Rhena and herself, his daughter standing alongside her seated mother and staring determinedly into the camera. It was a very serious pose, but also a delightful extra that lightened his mood a little.

His daughter was growing up so quickly, and seemed a lot older than the last image he had received. She looked very much like Helene. Schweitzer sighed as he gave his moustache a good tug. His mission here had overruled his personal life. This had been agreed with Helene, but it did not make it any easier.

There had been two violent acts at or near Lambaréné, and that worried him greatly. Violence had always been abhorrent to him. It had been since early childhood, and this viewpoint underpinned his faith.

Each incident had involved Adam Hope, a man he had immediately liked, but who had complicated issues and a lot of baggage with him.

One white man attacking another here was ghastly, but would it have been thus if it were two black men? Schweitzer liked to think so, but he sucked hard on his pipe as he searched his mind for answers, searched his soul indeed. Sometimes, when conditions at Lambaréné became so difficult, it felt as if his whole *zeitgeist* was being challenged.

He could not think of a better word for it in French, let alone English.

At times like this he felt he was at a crossroads. On one road were the old ways and beliefs that had always sustained him, and on the other the new ideas that were creeping into western society. The new ideas that people like Amie Moreau preached. Maybe Adam Hope shared them too, though that one was far more tight-lipped about his life and his beliefs.

Outside the storm was still raging. It's what the English call a second wind, Schweitzer thought, pleased with his pun. Occasionally he thought in English, and even more so in French.

Schweitzer could hear the wind that supported the rain trying to find any chink in the house to attack, and there were many. Fittings were whistling and creaking everywhere. There would have to be a thorough check on all the buildings when this season of storms was over, especially the hospital. A roof leaking mid-surgery was something he had experienced before.

Schweitzer put Helene's letter with the others, in the small cherrywood box he kept in his bureau. The problem of Pieters now occupied his mind. It was more pressing than Adam Hope. He would need a second pipe to think about it, so he diligently prepared a fresh one. No man was beyond salvation, but the Belgian would present a formidable challenge.

*

I sat in my *River Ghost* cabin, trying to work out if I could survive on the money I had left. Whenever I did my accounting, my mind constantly wandered. As a businessman

I was a fraud, for despite my eye for a profit, money had never really meant that much to me. This probably made me a traitor in the eyes of my fellow traders, but that didn't trouble me at all.

I had bruises all over my body from the battering the river had given me, but I'd had no reaction from any water I might have swallowed. Schweitzer said that if I didn't get ill within twenty-four hours I was probably in the clear. He also said the blow to the head had done no lasting damage. It seemed that Hope was still lucky, and Schweitzer had allowed me to leave his hospital earlier today.

I felt the boat bump and sway under me. The river was still swelling up. It would be a bloated expanse twice its size when the rains finished. That was the best time for logs to be floated down river to the coast. At least a dozen men would be on each raft, all polling desperately as the river tried to dislodge them. It was a dangerous business, but currently the only way to transport logs.

Gabon was basically one large swamp and I doubted that railways would ever be feasible here. That meant that any trees cut down had to be close to the river. Even trees just a mile from water were impossible to move.

I lit up a cheap cigar and wondered when I'd next be able to afford a case of Havanas. I craved a glass of something to go with the smoke. Where was Penaud when I needed him?

There was a light knock on the door.

'Come in,' I said, expecting to see Julius.

Amie entered.

'There was no one around on deck so I just came aboard,' she said.

Amie looked as fresh as the day was heavy. She was wearing a light blue dress that matched the patch of sky I could see through the cabin porthole. Blue seemed to be her colour.

'There should have been someone on watch, but my men are probably all lounging around somewhere,' I said, as I instinctively tried to tidy up the mess on my small desk.

'Do I still make you nervous, Adam?'

'A bit. You know people will talk, you coming on board unescorted like this.'

'Let them.'

Amie leant forward to kiss me, running a hand through my hair as she did so.

'Well, I don't want you to be nervous any more,' she said.

Amie started to undress, and the way she did it seemed the most natural thing in the world. She beckoned me towards her.

An hour later there was another knock on the door, this time a sharp rap. I quickly put on a tattered old dressing gown that had survived the trenches with me as the face of Julius presented itself. He was grinning from ear to ear, showing a fine array of white teeth. I blocked the doorway, but he knew very well that Amie was inside.

'Sorry, boss,' Julius said, 'the doctor man says for you to come to his house. Big problem, he says.'

'Okay. Where are the rest of the men? There was no one on deck.'

'I know, boss.'

'Well, where the hell are they?'

Julius shrugged.

'I hope they haven't found any booze.'

'No drink here, boss. And no gambling, because they don't have no money.'

'All right, but you go and find them and get them back on board, and tell Dr. Schweitzer I'll be with him shortly.'

'This will be all over the camp by tonight,' I said as I shut the door.

'Oh well, wasn't it worth it?'

Amie had propped herself up in the bunk, a thin sheen of sweat coating her body. She knew I wanted her again.

'I'd better go to see what Schweitzer wants,' I said. 'It sounds urgent.'

'I'll stay here, then. I need to catch up on some sleep, and this bunk is quite comfortable — for one.'

I dressed as quickly as I could, then poured out some tepid water from a jug to wash my face. As I was about to leave Amie asked how I felt.

'I feel like I'm a long way from Cardiff,' I said.

*

Schweitzer sat at his piano with the cat at his feet. The cat was looking for a chance to jump up on his lap. It usually did when he played. Sebastian saw the piano as a rival. Schweitzer played a few short pieces but his muse was absent this day, and did not invite him into the music. Eventually he stopped, and his hands just rested on the keyboard.

Joseph knocked and entered the room, which was rare for him. Usually he waited until he heard the doctor's voice. Joseph had an agitated Galoan tribesman with him.

'Is something the matter, Joseph?' Schweitzer said.

'Yes, sir. Big matter.'

The Galoan started to talk loudly, barely taking breath.

'Joseph, you'll have to translate what this man is saying, and please tell him to calm down.'

The man spoke of a great disaster that had befallen his village. It had been swamped with ants, millions of them. All their fowl and small animals had been killed and eaten, and the only thing the people could do there was to escape themselves, leaving their village to its fate.

The tribesman said the ants were coming directly towards Lambaréné. Countless millions had been energised by the rains and were now on the march. The man tried to make a rough diagram on Schweitzer's kitchen table, tracing parallel lines with his thumb, and then jabbing it into the centre of the table, which was Lambaréné.

'We all have to go,' Joseph said. 'Can't stay here now.'

'Ask this man how long before the ants arrive?'

'He says two days, sir, but maybe come quicker. They go very fast. Eat everything.'

Schweitzer knew that leaving Lambaréné was not an option, but he kept his counsel, for now.

'Thank this man and see that he has food and shelter.'

It was disturbing news, and the last thing Schweitzer needed after recent events. In his first time at Lambaréné, he had heard tales of the traveller ant, and the havoc it could cause. They marched twice a year, at the start and end of the wet season. There could be as many as fifty million of them, moving in destructive columns, and each one eating its way to its destination. Even trees were scaled, so that the huge spiders that lived there could be devoured. For many years they had taken a route close to Lambaréné, but not close enough to cause any danger. If the tribesman was right, this time they were heading straight for it.

For the first time in his life Schweitzer felt something approaching panic, because abandoning Lambaréné was not an option. Where would they all go? And the very sick, men like Pieters, could not be moved. All the hens would perish, and many other creatures here. How could such a multitude be kept out?

'You too will be in great danger,' Schweitzer muttered, as he ruffled the cat's head. He played the piano again, for he needed the comfort it brought him, and Sebastian got his way, deftly jumping up when he thought Schweitzer wouldn't notice.

*

As I walked towards the sound of the piano I thought how strange it was too hear such exquisite playing in such a place. A brief frisson of old ways and old lives passed over me. If ever someone could be struck with regret, guilt and loneliness in one moment, I was that man. The music stopped, just as I was about to enter the house.

Schweitzer was waiting for me at the piano, with his contented cat on his lap. For a moment I thought he had fallen asleep, for his head was sinking down towards his chest and his eyes were almost closed. I wondered how many hours he worked each day.

'Ah, Mr. Hope, thank you for coming. I hope I didn't disturb you with my request?'

'Not at all.'

Schweitzer put down the cat and ran a hand over the keys of the piano, as if he was bidding it farewell.

'Music gives a soul to the universe, wings to the mind, flight to the imagination, and life to everything. That was said a long long time ago, Mr. Hope.'

'By whom?'

'Plato, would you believe? But there were no pianos in his time. Did you study the great philosophers?'

'Not in any depth. I might have, if I had gone to Oxford, but the war got in the way.'

'Quite, but many young men took up their studies again afterwards, the ones that survived.'

'Indeed they did, but not me.'

I expected to be asked why, but Schweitzer just opened his eyes fully and gave me that quizzical look of his. I felt he could see right inside me and know all that was there, as if he was probing the skull beneath the skin.

'What did you want to see me about, Doctor?'

'A serious matter indeed. What do you know about ants?'

'Ants?'

'Yes, Traveller ants to be precise. I've been told columns of them are on the march towards Lambaréné, countless millions of them. I've heard tales about them of course, but they have never come close to us before. I thought they were a problem for the creatures of the jungle, but never for Lambaréné.'

'Who's told you this?'

'A Galoan man from upriver.'

'And you believe him?'

'Yes I do. His village has been decimated, and his fear and despair were very real.'

I sat down in the chair Schweitzer offered. Oh yes, I knew all about the traveller ant all right. On the march they could be quite deadly, and if they were heading for Lambaréné dead centre there was a real problem.

'If that tribesman is right I'd say you have something of a crisis.'

'That's what I thought.'

'The *Alemba* and my *River Ghost* can take you out of here. Or we could stay on the river until they passed through Lambaréné.'

'What would be left of my hospital, and all my work here?'

'Well the ants don't eat things, just flesh and bone.'

'How dangerous are they to humans?'

'Very, if you don't get well out of their way. If someone old and infirm, or perhaps even a drunkard, fell down in their path, it would be fatal. They'd swarm all over a person, and a thousand ant stings acts as an instant anaesthetic. You'd soon become a carcass to be quickly eaten.'

Unexpectedly, Schweitzer reached out a hand and touched one of mine.

'Some of my patients could not be evacuated. Mr. Hope, Adam, do you know what else can be done? Can the ants be stopped?'

I took my time in answering.

'Maybe there is a way, but I've never put it to the test. Are you absolutely sure some of your patients cannot be moved?'

'I am.'

'When are the ants expected?'

'The man said two days. Maybe sooner.'

'We have no time to lose, then. Do you have kerosene here?'

'Kerosene?'

'Yes, maybe you call it paraffin.'

'Of course, we use it for all the lamps. I buy it in bulk, it's cheaper that way.'

'Good, I'll need all you have. I have some on board the *River Ghost*, and Penaud will have more.'

'But why?'

'They say the ants won't go near the stuff, but as I said, I've never put it to the test. We'll need all the men we can get. Hopefully I'll get Penaud on board with this, but you can never tell with him.'

'Oh, I think Captain Penaud is a decent man. He just likes to hide it under a layer of indifference.'

'I'll get back to the boats to tell him the news, then.'

'What do we need all the men for, as you say?'

'We'll have to build our defences. We need to dig trenches, create a moat around Lambaréné as much as we can, and fill it with kerosene.'

'Surely we won't have enough to do that.'

'No, but hopefully we have just enough to put down to deter the ants. It's the smell that will be vital, not the actual amount of fuel we use.'

I went back to the *River Ghost*, to find Amie fast asleep. I thought of waking her, but did not see the point. She looked so peaceful lying there. I took a minute just to look at her, the way she hugged the small bunk with her thin body. I closed the cabin door quietly and went to find Penaud. He was on the bridge of the *Alemba*, checking through some documents.

'God, how we French love forms,' he muttered when he saw me, 'but between you and me, I've learned to ignore most of them.'

Penaud offered me one of his broadest smiles.

'So, how are today, Adam? And how's the lovely Amie?'

So he knew. Of course he did, as did most of the camp. Schweitzer did too, probably, but he had been far too discreet to mention it.

I told Penaud the news about the ants and his mood quickly changed.

'They have always marched at least ten miles to the east of Lambaréné,' Penaud said, 'through the heart of the forest.'

'Not this time.'

'Well my first thought is to beat a hasty retreat down river. I'm only waiting here until Pieters is well enough to travel. Are you staying?'

'I am.'

I told Penaud about the kerosene plan as he marched around the bridge with his hands clasped behind his back. Very Napoleon-like, I thought.

'*Merde!* I hate sudden changes in my routine,' Penaud said. 'I'm tempted to leave Pieters here and forget about the whole thing, especially if you are not going to press charges.' Penaud stopped pacing and turned to face me. 'After all, you are okay, and Pieters is out of action. Well, *are* you going to press charges?'

'No — as you said, too much form filling. Pieters was out of his head anyway, even if he did almost kill me. If you remove him from Gabon, that will be enough for me.'

'So there's nothing keeping me here, then?'

'Nothing at all.'

Penaud started his journey around the bridge again.

'Damned morality,' Penaud murmured. 'I hope Schweitzer isn't inspiring you to be heroic, Adam? I've never liked heroes. They are dangerous.'

'I'm just doing what needs to be done. You can steam away if you want, but leave me what kerosene you have.'

'And have people say that I ran when you stayed? No thanks. As a representative of my wonderful French government I'll stay, but your plans had better damned work. What do you want the *Alemba* crew to do? Give me your orders, *Captain* Hope.'

Alemba's men joined with mine to make a crew of twelve, and Julius automatically took charge of them, barking orders left, right and centre. Penaud's main man objected, but not enough to challenge Julius. The amalgamated crew were an impressive physical bunch, their bodies honed from years of stoking boilers, and other hard labour.

Within an hour I had marked out a defensive perimeter for the camp, and the men began to dig a thin trench all around the main buildings of Lambaréné, which were the hospital, the school, and Schweitzer's house.

They were soon all singing away, which was a help to all of us. At this moment I felt at home here, thousands of miles away from Wales. At last I had a purpose, and a woman.

Schweitzer and Gillespie took no part in these preparations. They were busy in the hospital surgery, still caring for their patents, whilst all around them was descending into chaos. I hoped I could make it an ordered chaos.

Satisfied that the work was being done correctly, I started to organise the collection of kerosene. Joseph and various other Lambaréné residents helped with this. We began to stack up cans into a pyramid on what I hoped would be on the safe side of the trenches. Then I went down to the riverside, to secure what fuel the boats had.

On board the *River Ghost* a still sleepy Amie greeted me from the deck.

'What the hell is going on?' she said. 'What is everyone doing?'

I explained it to her as quickly and as calmly as I could.

'I don't like to even think about those ants,' she said. 'I've never liked any insect, really.'

'Well, you've sure come to the worst place, then.'

'I know, but if I hadn't I wouldn't have met you.'

'At least you'll have a vivid story for your book.'

'Oh, that. It's rapidly going out of my mind. What can I do to help?'

'Um.'

'You are not thinking that I'm the kind of woman who should hide behind the men, are you?'

'I wouldn't dare. Okay, find Joseph, detach him from the other workers, and tell him to prepare food for everyone. I know my men will build up a mighty hunger. I'm hungry myself, come to think of it. This will be a very tiring day.'

'Well, you've already been active.'

Amie laughed, and kissed me lightly on the cheek before striding off towards the centre of the action. I went below deck to lug up what cans of kerosene I had, and would then do the same on the *Alemba*. I hoped we had enough. It had to be enough.

*

Pieters could hear noise all around him. Men were shouting, and people running around outside. He could not remember much after he'd knocked Hope overboard, but that bastard had to be dead now, falling into the river like he did. The thought made him feel good, real good. It was payback for the arm, and he could rest easy now.

Pieters sat up carefully. He saw that he had fresh bandages, and the side of his face hurt, but he could feel his strength coming back. His fever was gone, and he felt more alert. There was a jug of water by the bed and a mug, but he just drank greedily from the jug. He heard someone outside the door and sank back down in the bed again to feign sleep. Now that Hope was dead his one thought was to get away. How he did it would need some thought before it got dark. Night came quickly in the forest, and night was always good for a man like him.

*

Gillespie joined Amie as she tried to organise food for so many. Joseph was reluctant to take orders from a woman, white or not, but changed his attitude when he saw Gillespie.

'Can I help you, miss?' Gillespie said.

Amie liked Gillespie. He had a quiet sense of decency, and none of the danger that Adam presented. None of the excitement either. Men like Gillespie made good friend material.

'I think it's all in hand now, Mr. Gillespie, but thank you.'

Gillespie looked exhausted. His young, earnest face was already creased with lines that would never be erased. The Gabon sun would make sure of that.

'Has the doctor finished surgery?' Amie said.

'Yes. It was routine stuff today. We're sending patients fit enough to walk a few miles inland, to the logging camp there. They will be out of the eye of the storm then, as it were. We'll have to protect the ones too sick too move as best we can. I trust your Mr. Hope knows what he is doing?'

'I'm sure he does,' Amie said, putting as much conviction into her voice as she could. She loved Gillespie's use of the word *your,* and hoped she didn't blush.

'I'd better help the doctor clean up,' Gillespie said, 'and then we'll both help with the digging.'

'You'll do no such thing, Mr. Gillespie. Dr. Schweitzer and yourself are far more valuable in the hospital.'

Amie joined in with Joseph and two other kitchen hands, and between them they managed to organise the chaos there. Giant-size bowls of spicy hot food were prepared. The men preparing the trenches would have to share the bowls, and dig into them the best they could.

Amie didn't really want to be in the kitchen, doing women's work. She wanted to be on the front line with the men, but she knew now was not the time. Even for women like her it would not be the time for many years. She was resigned to it, but in Paris she'd read of the efforts of the English suffragettes, and had been inspired. Her French sisters were some way behind.

*

All the kerosene I could find had been rounded up. The pyramid of large cans looked impressive enough, but whether it would work was anyone's guess.

Penaud approached me. He was soaked through with sweat, but he still had his official dark blue naval coat on. It seemed like he was bonded to it.

'I'm too old for this,' Penaud said, dabbing at his brow.

'Don't tell me you've been digging, Penaud?'

'Of course not. My commitment only goes so far, but it's damned hard work trying to control the men. Some of them want to bolt back to the *Alemba* and hide.'

I looked up at the leaden skies above me.

'We'd better pray that the rains hold off,' I said.

'Why?'

'Because a downpour would dilute the smell of the kerosene, maybe to a fatal degree.'

'Well, talking of prayers, here's the right man for them, and he's heading our way.'

Schweitzer joined us. For once the doctor was not in good sartorial condition. His clothes were mud-spattered and his hair was awry, sticking up in tufts on his head. Even his moustache looked somewhat dishevelled.

'How are our defences coming along?' Schweitzer said.

'The trenches are mainly dug now. We have to continue one around the back of your house, but the hospital has been secured.'

'We have a long way to go yet, Doctor,' Penaud said. 'We are in the lap of the gods, you might say.'

'I prefer to make my God singular,' Schweitzer said.

'Amie is helping Joseph organise food for everyone,' I said.

'Yes, so Gillespie has told me. I'm sure your men could use it. They are working so hard.'

'Fear is a powerful motive,' Penaud said.

'Come, come, Captain Penaud, you spread your scepticism too thickly.'

'Yes, I'm afraid that sometimes I do. I'm sorry, Doctor.'

Two tribesmen were quickly approaching us, almost running. I tensed, as very recent memories came flooding back. Schweitzer said one was the same man who had brought the news about the ants. Joseph was following on behind them. He was so excited he forgot his French and started talking rapidly in Galoan until Schweitzer calmed him down.

The new man said that the ants were now advancing at what was a breakneck speed, for them.

'Man say ants here by tonight, sir,' Joseph said. 'Attack us in dark.'

Joseph clutched at Schweitzer's arm. 'We should go. All go on big boats.'

'Calm yourself, Joseph. Never forget God is watching over us. With His help we shall stay.'

'Maybe it's not such a bad thing,' I said. 'The sooner we face them the better.'

'Yes, whilst our nerve holds,' Penaud said quietly.

'How can I help?' Schweitzer said.

'I think it will be best if you and Gillespie stay in the hospital. With what is to come, I'm sure your patients there will be glad of your presence and your strength, Doctor. Don't worry: if we need you, I'll let you know.'

'Are you sure, Mr. Hope?'

'Yes. It's best to let us get on now.'

Schweitzer put a hand on my shoulder.

'We are in your debt. Oh, and yours too, Penaud.'

'I'm just doing what needs to be done, Doctor, and don't thank me yet. I'm not certain this is going to work.'

'I have faith. I'll go back to the hospital, then, tend to my flock, as it were. Please make sure that each of you gets food and drink.'

'Did he mention drink?' Penaud said, when Schweitzer was out of earshot.

'Not the type you want, Penaud. Right, can you see that the trench behind the doctor's house is finished now, and make sure there are no gaps at all in it. Any gap in our line and they'll pour through it.'

'Aye aye, Captain Hope.'

'And tell your men to go the kitchen in the house when they are finished. There should be food waiting for them by now.'

'It's all kicking back in, isn't it, Adam?'

'What is?'

'Your army training. What you learnt in the war. You've become a real captain again, not some blurred man that plays about on a riverboat.'

'You really do talk too much, Penaud.'

196

'Of course I do. It's one of the few pleasures I have left, *mon ami*.'

Penaud disappeared, taking a few of his men with him.

I shouted for Julius and he quickly appeared. He was bare-chested and shining. His torso was rippled with muscle tone, but not so it detracted from his leanness.

'What you want, boss?'

'Julius, I haven't had time to thank you for what you did for me.'

'Julius glad to do it, boss, but the French captain should have let me kill that Pieters man.'

I stretched out a hand for Julius to shake. He stepped back, confused, but I kept me hand out. Julius took it, at first hesitantly, then shaking it vigorously until I detached it.

'I need you to help me again now,' I said. 'You are the best man for it.'

I explained what we were going to do with the kerosene, and that timing was everything. If we put it down too soon before the ants arrived it might lose its effect; too late and disaster would strike. And then there was the rain to worry about. We needed a lot of luck, or Schweitzer's God on our side.

'Tell a few of the men to collect up all the doctor's hens. Look, they're wandering all over the place. Gather them up and lock them in their shed, or they'll be food for the ants. Then tell the men to go to the kitchen, where they will be fed.'

If kerosene-soaked trenches were not enough there was one last thing I could try, a final throw of the dice, but I thought it best to keep that to myself for now. There was only so much the harassed men could take in. I could sense fear all around me, and it would only escalate as night fell. It was already getting close to dusk. Our wills were about to be tested.

Penaud was right. Old instincts had come back, and I liked the feeling. This was a time for action, not contemplation. I had done far too much of that in recent years.

I thought we had enough kerosene to soak the trenches, but I knew the ants would probe everywhere for a weakness. On the march they were a magnificent army, led by their shock troops, the soldier ants. These would try to pour into Lambaréné first, stinging everything that moved, and thus preparing the ground for the main body.

I told Julius to split up our hoard of cans so that each section of the trenches had a few ready, and a man that knew how to use them.

'One man for each can, but not to be opened until I signal it.'

'Yes, boss.'

'I'm going up to the kitchen now. Tell all the men who have been digging to come too, but not all at once. Two at a time. You're in charge now, Julius.'

'Yes, we all have empty bellies, boss.'

'I know.'

Amie was sitting at the long table in the kitchen. I was impressed by the array of large bowls and basins that had been filled with everything she could find.

'Hello, Amie.'

She got up quickly and ran to hold me, oblivious to the stares of everyone else there.

'You've done well,' I said, gently pushing her away.

'Have *you*? Outside, I mean.'

'The trenches have been dug and the kerosene readied.'

'It will be dark in half an hour.'

'Yes, but men have been posted just outside the perimeter. They'll be lighting fires anytime now. We'll need a few inside our perimeter too, or we'll have difficulty in seeing what's happening.'

'Do you want to eat, Adam?'

'Of course. Let me at it.'

'I've sent some across for the doctor and Gillespie.'

'Have you, now? You'd make a very good soldier.'

'I want to kiss you,' Amie whispered.

'Well you'd better not. Don't you know I'm an officer? Not sure about the gentleman part.'

'Good God, did you just try to make a joke?'

Two men squabbling over the same bowl caught our attention, which was probably a good thing.

Penaud joined us as I was shovelling down food.

'We'll be starting to lose the light soon,' he said.

'Yes. Did you finish that trench?'

'Yes, everything is secured that can be. Ah, food — is there any left for me?'

'Sit down and I'll fix you up a mixed bowl,' Amie said.

'I'll leave you to it, Penaud. I want to make a final check with Julius.'

Penaud was right about the light. The last yellow streaks of it were fading over the forest, leaving the sky a darkening grey. Night would come quickly now. An unnatural stillness had come over Lambaréné. Where were the birds? Their usual dusk chatter was absent. They knew something was amiss. Birds always did.

The men outside the perimeter had lit a few small fires, clusters of light that increased as the skies darkened. Other men were doing the same inside what I hoped would be our safety zone.

I began to feel the same kind of tension I had felt in France, waiting for our barrage to cease and whistles to be blown up and down the line. Then that awful trudge towards the enemy as their Maxims opened up, every type of hellish sound ringing in my ears. We were like British redcoats marching in formation towards the guns of the other side. Nothing much had changed in a hundred years in 1914, apart from the colour of the uniforms.

I made a final check of our trench defences. They did not look much, but would have to do. I had arranged the cans of kerosene as best I could, but whether we had enough was anyone's guess. The ants would probe for any weakness they could find, honed by instinct and the need for food.

Penaud was having a last cigar before the attack started.

'Have you got another one of those?' I asked.

'Alas no, my friend. Unless you want me to get more from the *Alemba*.'

'We don't have time for that.'

'Here, have a pull on mine.'

I took the cigar from him and had a long drag.

'Calms the nerves, doesn't it?'

I didn't have time to answer for the men stationed outside the camp were running back, most of them crying out their warnings.

'They come, boss,' Julius shouted. 'Ants come.'

'Tell the men to hold up their torches close to the trenches,' I shouted. 'We need as much light as possible, and Julius, Penaud, now is the time to put down the kerosene.'

All around our defences our men emptied cans into the trenches, and the night air was filled with the pungent smell of the fuel. I could see the first ants now, approaching us like a long dark shadow. These would be the soldier ants, the assault force for the main body.

The hens in their shed started up a frightful clucking. If the ants broke in en masse these would be the first to perish, their nostrils filled until they suffocated, and their carcasses picked clean in minutes.

Despite our best efforts, some of the ants did get through our defences. They were not much bigger than European ants, but they had much stronger jaws and moved at greater speed. I felt the first nip at my ankle and shook a cluster from my legs. Yelps rose up from everywhere as I moved amongst the men, cajoling, bullying, making sure the liquid was spread evenly around the trenches, and that everyone was on the safe side of them.

The main body of ants arrived. A quivering, massed threat was moving towards us like a vast, undulating snake. I knew it was time for my final gambit.

'Now's the time to light the trenches!' I shouted. 'C'mon, light them up everywhere.'

I snatched up a torch and started the action myself, and was soon followed by others as the trenches began to smoke. Kerosene was not so inflammable as petrol, but it would burn longer.

The ants swirled in one direction then the other, like random waves lapping up against a shoreline, but each time our fiery trenches baulked most of them. Even the ants' hunger could not conquer their hatred of the smell of burning kerosene.

The soldier ants that did manage to get in still numbered in the thousands, and they were pricking my body everywhere. I could feel parts of it starting to numb. This was how they worked on big animals, biting until the beasts were so stunned by pain they fell. I shook them off the best I could.

It struck me what a strange scene this was for Schweitzer's world. Torches lighting up the sky, black, glistening figures running around, channels of evil-smelling liquid coruscating in the lurid light. It was as if the Devil had come to visit Schweitzer's world. The attack could not have lasted much more than ten minutes, but it seemed like an eternity.

Penaud appeared alongside me, doing a small St. Vitas-like dance as he tried to brush ants off him.

'These damn things really bite,' he shouted.

'Be glad only a tiny faction of them have got in. You'll survive, Penaud. Think of all the tales you can tell down on the coast. By next year it will all be about how you saved Lambaréné.'

'Yes, I like the sound of that.'

'If it *is* saved.'

I saw that the fire in the trenches was dying down as the kerosene burnt out. This was a crucial moment, but suddenly the main body of ants veered away from us, just as quickly as they had arrived. It looked like they had given up, and that their one collective will had been thwarted. A ragged cheer went up from the camp as the ants disappeared into the forest. Finally we were safe.

*

Pieters seemed to be in the midst of chaos. At first he thought it was inside his head, wild sounds reverberating there, all stoking up his hate. It took him a few minutes to sit upright in the bed, wincing as the pain of his wound shot through him once again. There seemed no end to it. He could see the light of many fires outside. People were running around everywhere, and most of them were shouting.

Pieters dressed as well as he could and got up, carefully. He felt light-headed, but managed to stay upright. He opened the door to his room. There was no one around, which surprised him. He would have thought Penaud would have at least stationed a man on the door, but that was the fool's mistake.

All his thoughts were focused on getting away now. He knew if the French started digging into his past all kinds of things might come up to add to the murder of Hope. He knew they'd send him across the water for sure, and no one ever came back from Devil's Island.

His plan was to get to a dugout and drift downstream. If he could get to the coast he had a chance of getting away. There were still a few people there who owed him favours. He crushed out the thought of a one-armed wounded man being alone in a dugout on the Ogowe.

Pieters edged out into the night, keeping his back against the hospital wall. What the hell was going on here? It seemed like a pagan festival, but at Lambaréné? Men passed close by him, shouting out stuff in Galoan, but he only knew a few words of that. He could see bursts of light all around him from the multiple fires, and the whole camp stank of kerosene. Whatever was happening, this madness suited him.

Pieters edged out into the part of Lambaréné that was the darkest. He kept to the shadows as much as he could, and struggled over a narrow trench that someone had dug. It stank even more of fuel but that didn't bother him as he pushed himself into the undergrowth beyond. Men appeared at the trench with torches and suddenly it was alight. Pieters could smell kerosene burning. Had everyone gone mad here?

Pieters saw Hope. He blinked hard, and blinked again. He must be seeing things, still affected by his fever. He took a deep breath and stared, screwing up his eyes in concentration. It *was* Hope. The man was about fifty metres away and looked to be directing the firing of the trenches. The bastard was still alive.

Pieters felt like someone had a hold of his guts and was trying to wrench them from him. It made him feel the loss of his arm all the more. Hope looked none the worse for the blow on his head and his fall into the river. How the hell had the man survived that? They did not call him Lucky Hope for nothing.

Pieters tried to think. He had to get away and stay alive; then there might be another chance of revenge. Yes, that was it. He had to keep his powder dry for another day. Getting away must be his priority now. Hope's time would come later. He'd missed out on his own father but he'd make sure he'd get Hope, one day.

Crouching down, Pieters began to make his way towards the river. He kept to the undergrowth on the outskirts of the camp, away from the burning trenches and the choking smell of kerosene. So much was going on, he doubted that anyone would even notice him.

Something nipped at his ankles. He shook off a few ants, cursing the jungle as he did so. He heard a strange sound, one that seemed to be encircling him. It was a different noise to what was going on in the camp. This was a swirling, clicking sound that he could not identify. Shadows seemed to be moving all around him. Instinct told him to move away from them as quickly as he could, but he tripped on a tree root and went down on the stump of his arm.

As he yelled out in pain the ants were on him in seconds. They were crazed by the smell of the blood, and they quickly found its source. He felt his body start to quiver as they engulfed him, covering him in seconds. Pieters tried to scream but the ants filled his gasping mouth before he could. No sound came from him after that, and the ants, thwarted by the burning trenches, had their night.

*

In the aftermath of the battle Schweitzer sought me out, walking towards me through the smoke in that determined stride of his.

'We owe you Lambaréné,' Schweitzer said. 'We would surely have been overrun.'

'We could have sheltered a lot of people on the two boats.'

'Don't belittle what you have done for us, Adam. We could never have moved the sick in time, and my work here would have been ruined once again. Come to the surgery, please. I think you have been quite badly bitten.'

As Schweitzer tended the many stings on my calves I thought of Amie and the life we might have together. I went to look for her as soon as Schweitzer was finished. She was still in the kitchen, but it was now empty, of people and most of the food. She had her back to me when I quietly entered, but I could see how tired she was by the slump of her shoulders.

'It looks like we came through it,' I said.

Amie dropped the bowl she was cleaning and it shattered on the floor.

'Damn, look what you made me do. Don't creep up on me like that.'

'Sorry.'

We held each other as tightly as we could.

'What a day,' Amie murmured.

'Yes indeed, in more ways than one.'

Even after the last ten hours Amie still smelt good. She had a light and airy fragrance that belied all the work she must have been doing in the kitchen.

'Well, the woman was stuck with the cooking again,' Amie murmured, her face still pushed hard into my chest.

'At least you didn't say *little* woman.'

'I hope we live to be very old,' Amie said, 'long enough to see real change.'

'For women?'

'Of course, but change in so many other way too. Most of the people out here, the whites that is, have the same views their grandparents had.'

'Maybe the war has started to change all that.'

'Maybe.'

'I'm going back to the *River Ghost*, Adam, I need to rest.'

'Okay. I'll join you soon.'

I explored Lambaréné, stepping carefully amongst the blackened trenches. It was hard to come down from the adrenalin rush of the ants' attack. My thoughts were darting everywhere. I recalled my first trip into the hinterland of the Ogowe, the *River Ghost* bumping against the bank as I moored up into the unknown. I was a novice captain then, and everything was new, and as intimidating as it was exciting.

Men had lined up for their worthless rum, and it dawned on me now what had shone out of their staring eyes. Pity. Pity for the way they were, and pity for the way I was. One man had seemed to look into my very soul, and, even when he took his bottle, his look said that he was a better man than me.

I sat on the veranda of Schweitzer's house, trying to collect my thoughts. All the fires were out now, but a low-lying cloud of pungent smoke hung over the camp. It was the aftermath to a battle smell, one that I knew all too well from the war.

Lambaréné was alive with jungle noises again, as my exhausted men headed for their bunks. Night creatures were taking back control of their world, letting us know that they had always been here, long before us.

Schweitzer joined me after a while. We smoked and looked out onto the Ogowe. The river that had almost claimed me was in full flood now. It caught the moon on its surface and threw it back at a sky iridescent with stars. They were bright enough to shine through the smoke that hung everywhere over the camp. We watched it slowly drift up and away into the night.

I could feel the doctor's eyes on me.

'The calm after the storm,' Schweitzer said.

'Indeed.'

'When the sky is alive with stars like this I always feel small, just a tiny speck of humanity.'

'There's nothing small about you, Doctor.'

'Might I ask what you think of my work here, Adam?'

'It's a remarkable achievement.'

'From some men I would see that as a platitude, but not you.'

'Good, because it was heartfelt.'

'I prefer to say my progress is steady, but—'

Schweitzer stopped in mid sentence, holding his pipe in one hand and tugging at his moustache with the other.

'Is something on your mind, Doctor?'

'Always, always, my boy. God has given me a path to follow, but the way is not easy. Don't worry, I'm not about to give you a lecture.'

'But something *is* on your mind?'

'Amie Moreau thinks that I don't treat the people here as equals. She is wrong, because we are all equal in the eyes of God, but I do see the black man here as my junior brother.'

'Why is that?'

'I think a slow development is needed here, not a headlong rush into new ways. How long has it taken Europe to develop? Two thousand years ago it was Godless, and just centuries ago people were still being burnt for saying the earth went round the sun. Yet we come to places like Gabon and expect them to suddenly change, whilst taking so much from them.'

'But do we really have anything better to offer them? Millions of people, white people, have been killed in *our* war. That hardly puts us in a position of moral superiority.'

'To be sure, but at least I offer them God, and an improvement in their physical well-being. I hope people will judge me on that, if they judge me at all.'

Schweitzer attended to his pipe. It seemed to be a part of the man. He stoked it up, sending a shower of sparks out into the night. For a moment they seemed like a small burst of stars falling from the sky.

'What of you, Adam? Like most here you bear the mark of pain,' Schweitzer murmured softly.

'What's that?'

'Men endure extremes of bodily and mental torment, but to suffer them and then be freed, that's one of the things that makes life so precious. So, are you beginning to feel free, Adam?'

'I don't know much about such matters.'

'Oh, I think that you do. I think you know a great deal about such matters, and never so clearly as now. And most of your life is ahead of you.'

'Why did you accept me here so readily? I doubt that any of your colleagues would approve, even before the shooting.'

'I make up my own mind about a man. *He who saves a single soul saves the world entire.* Do you know the line? It is from the Talmud — the Hebrew bible. It came to me when I treated your legs.'

'I'm not familiar with it.'

I could not think of anything more to say to Schweitzer. I don't think any more words were expected. I wondered if his work here would be lauded by future generations, or whether history would bury him as an anachronism, with outdated ideas. His junior brother quote would not go down with Amie. I felt uncomfortable with it myself, but there was far more to the man than Victorian traits.

We sat quietly for a while, each of us lost in our thoughts, until Schweitzer knocked the ash from his pipe and bade me goodnight. His eyes were still bright, despite the chronic fatigue his body must be feeling. I wondered if I would ever see the man again.

As I walked down towards the river I was surprised by how calm I was, such an amazing calmness. There seemed to be a sudden easing of ten years of pain, as if an escape valve had been opened, and all the bile of my past life was running out through it. There was relief too, relief that had not been there when Armistice Day finally came. Then there had been just a wretched, gnawing emptiness, a feeling that nothing had really been achieved, apart from four years of bloody slaughter. I'd felt like I was a shell of a man, someone who had been hollowed out from the inside and left empty. I remember Lucky Hope being unable to stop the flow of tears, and I was close to them now. I dabbed at my eyes as discreetly as I could.

I was hoping for a new future with Amie and thought I might sleep soundly tonight, but if the German boy did come, I would shake his hand and call *him* Kamerad.

For a few minutes I sat on a convenient stump by the river's edge, the remains of a tree that had been ruined by the incessant attack of water. The river that had almost taken me was still in full flow. Most of the year it was a grey expanse of water moving at a slow pace, one that matched the surrounding countryside, and the people in it. But it had its moods, and perhaps its sudden changes matched the ebb and flow of my life here. Long months of slow trading in the sun, an almost torpor-like existence at times, broken by sudden, unexpected, and tragic action. People like Pieters behaving in a way no one could ever have foreseen. I'd thought the Belgian a drunk and a man rough around the edges, but never capable of doing the things he had done. Perhaps all of us are locked inside with demons and forlorn hopes. Schweitzer had told me once that every man has his reasons, and I wondered what Pieters' were.

A fish broke the surface of the river close by me, an elegant flash of silver in the night. I took a last look at Lambaréné as I walked on to my steamboat. I had no doubt that Schweitzer's vision would remain true. The forest all around me was alive with sounds as night approached. Screeched warnings and cries blended into a common identity, and it seemed that I had never heard it so clearly.

I could see Amie waiting for me on the deck of the *River Ghost*. As I came into range of the deck light she saw me. She waved a hand, and I waved back.

Cockatrice Books
Y diawl a'm llaw chwith

The cockatrice is hatched from a cockerel's egg, and resembles a dragon the size and shape of a cockerel. The English word is derived from the Latin *calcatrix*, but in Welsh it is called *ceiliog neidr*: 'adder-cock.' Its touch, breath and glance are lethal.

There is a saying in Welsh, *Y ddraig goch ddyry cychwyn,* which means, 'The red dragon leads the way.' The cockatrice spits at your beery patriotism.

www.cockatrice-books.com

ANY KIND OF BROKEN MAN: COLLECTED STORIES
ROGER GRANELLI
with a foreword by Phil Rickman

A veteran of the war with Japan confronts the Japanese factory which has revivified his valley. An ageing Navajo on the edge of the desert meets his doctor son's white bride. A young jazz musician walks into a club with a pistol in his pocket, and a young criminal from the valleys who is suspected of murder finds peace of mind on a Scottish beach.

Grounded in the post-industrial communities of Wales, yet encompassing Spain, Malaysia and the Florida Keys, this collection spans the career of a prominent novelist from the early 1990s to the present day. Drug dealers, labourers, invalids and war criminals confront the start of a new century, the death of old certainties and old ways of life, the comforting weight of bitterness and the fearful beginnings beginnings of hope.

'Roger Granelli's books are incredibly hard to put down.'
The Big Issue

'His characters breathe, make you care. One day the people that count will realise that Roger Granelli is... the best un-sung novelist in Wales.'

Phil Rickman

FIVE GO TO SWITZERLAND AND OTHER STORIES
NIGEL JARRETT

A daughter curious about her widowed father's love life; a woman survivor of domestic abuse; a wife who learns something startling about her jazz-loving husband at his funeral; an old actor facing memory loss; a couple whose son was executed by militants; a black American academic on a stressful stay in Wordsworth country; an early 20th-century scullery maid being taught to read by a sinister manservant... and more.

In his fourth short-story collection, award-winning writer Nigel Jarrett disturbs the clear, slow-flowing waters of ordinary lives to reveal their complications and unresolved tensions.

'Here are vivid and vital stories that crackle like bushfire and ignite delight... I read them with unbridled pleasure and holy envy.'

Jon Gower

'Jarrett's stories take seemingly ordinary or innocent situations and gently tease out their emotional complexity.'

Lesley McDowell, *Independent on Sunday*

SEASIDE TOWNS

A. L. REYNOLDS

For Anatoliy Yetvushenko, émigré and physicist, it should be the perfect holiday. Llandudno calls to his mind the Black Sea holidays of his childhood in Ukraine, while his companion, Francis, is just beginning to awaken to the possibilities of male sexual love in the first years following its legalisation. But Anatoliy has memories of an earlier holiday in Lyme Regis in the 1950s, where his previous lover, who now lives near Llandudno, left him to make a loveless marriage. With its awareness of the landscape of the north coast of Wales, of quantum physics and of deep time, this novel reflects the search for intimacy and fulfilment in the shadow of political tyranny and sexual persecution.

'gentle yet searing, introspective yet intensely physical. A real gem of a book... Seek it out if you can.'

Rachel Rees, *Buzz Magazine*

'the wonder, the intensity, the profound gratitude of [sexual love]... the intimately human [cast] in an epic light, in the awesome interconnectedness of all'

Niall Griffiths, *Nation Cymru*

PUGNACIOUS LITTLE TROLLS
ROB MIMPRISS

In his first three short-story collections, Rob Mimpriss painstakingly mapped the unregarded lives of Welsh small-town and country-dwellers. In Pugnacious Little Trolls, he combines the skill and quiet eloquence of his earlier work with confident experimentation, with stories set among the bird-bodied harpies of Central America, among the dog-headed Cynocephali of Central Asia, among humanity's remote descendants at the very end of the universe, and in the muddle of slag-heaps and job centres that H. G. Wells' Country of the Blind has become. In the three stories at the heart of the collection is Tanwen, idealistic and timid, embarking on her adult life in the shadow of global warming and English nationalism.

Where is the Welsh short story going? Wherever Rob Mimpriss takes it.

John O'Donoghue

bathed in white fire in every sense... Borges would happily own them.

Gee Williams

freely and fiercely inventive short stories... supercharged with ideas

Jon Gower, *Nation Cymru*